Liz!

Heart pounding, Tim crouched on his snowboard, picking up speed. His gaze searched the downhill path. There! Liz, unmistakable in her pink ski jacket, lay facedown. A man loomed over her.

Tim let out a howl of rage. He didn't have time to think about words, just bellowed like a bear. An *angry* bear. If that man harmed one hair on Liz's head...

The guy let go. With lightning speed, he darted away. Tim shot across the snow in a direct path to his ex-fiancée. He threw himself to his knees on the snow beside her and gathered her up in his arms.

"There, baby. It's okay now. I won't let anything happen to you."

She threw her arms around his neck, her sobs loud in his ear.

In that instant, Tim knew. In fact, he'd *always* known.

He was still in love with her.

Books by Virginia Smith

Love Inspired Suspense

Murder by Mushroom
Bluegrass Peril
A Taste of Murder
Murder at Eagle Summit

VIRGINIA SMITH

A lifelong lover of books, Virginia Smith has always enjoyed immersing herself in fiction. In her mid-twenties she wrote her first story and discovered that writing well is harder than it looks; it took many years to produce a book worthy of publication. During the daylight hours she steadily climbed the corporate ladder and stole time late at night after the kids were in bed to write. With the publication of her first novel, she left her twenty-year corporate profession to devote her energy to her passion—writing stories that honor God and bring a smile to the faces of her readers. When she isn't writing, Ginny and her husband, Ted, enjoy exploring the extremes of nature—snow skiing in the mountains of Utah, motorcycle riding on the curvy roads of central Kentucky, and scuba diving in the warm waters of the Caribbean. Visit her online at www.VirginiaSmith.org.

VIRGINIA SMITH

Murder *at* EAGLE SUMMIT

Steeple
Hill®

Published by Steeple Hill Books™

STEEPLE HILL BOOKS

Steeple
Hill®

Recycling programs
for this product may
not exist in your area.

ISBN-13: 978-0-373-44335-2
ISBN-10:   0-373-44335-8

MURDER AT EAGLE SUMMIT

Copyright © 2009 by Virginia Smith

www.SteepleHill.com

Printed in U.S.A.

Cleanse me with hyssop, and I will be clean:
wash me, and I will be whiter than snow.
—*Psalms* 51:7

For my husband, Ted.

Thank you for introducing me to Utah skiing.

Acknowledgments

This story would not have come about if not for the assistance of many people. Thanks to:

Susan Ashley, who gave me the idea of setting a story in Park City, and for invaluable insights about the day-to-day operation of ski resorts. And for so many terrific ideas, like finding a frozen body on a chair lift.

Zach and Heidi Nakaishi, for patiently answering my questions and for educating me about police procedures in Utah's Summit County.
If I goofed it's not their fault.

Tracy Ruckman and Amy Barkman,
for excellent feedback.

The CWFI Critique Group for working so hard on the first few chapters, the summary, and title brainstorming: Amy S., Amy B., Vicki T., Sherry K., Richard L., Ann K. and Tracy R.

My agent, Wendy Lawton, for believing in me and telling me so.

Editor extraordinaire Krista Stroever, whose insights make me a better writer and whose encouragement makes me a grateful one.

And finally, thanks to my Lord Jesus, for more things than I could possibly list here. But He knows.

ONE

"Have you ever seen an uglier dress in your life?"

Liz Carmichael pitched her voice to be heard over the windshield wipers and the downpour of rain battering against the roof of the car. Rainfall this heavy was unusual in December, but nothing about this warm Kentucky winter could be called usual. She lifted her head from the passenger headrest and cracked one tired lid to see her friend's reaction to her question.

Jazzy clutched the wheel with both hands, her gaze fixed on the wet road through the windshield. Lightning flashed across the coal-black sky above them, illuminating her dainty profile in an eerie white glow.

"It was pretty awful," she agreed without looking toward Liz.

From the backseat came Caitlin's voice. "But the bride was beautiful."

"What bride?" Liz snorted. "If there was a girl somewhere inside all those ruffles, I couldn't see her."

"Oh, there was a bride, all right. I have her check to prove it." The corner of Jazzy's mouth twisted. "And a stiff neck, too."

"Yeah, and my lips are numb." Caitlin, the flutist in their classical ensemble, sounded tired, too. "I think that's the longest we've ever played at a wedding reception. We earned our money tonight, that's for sure."

Liz rubbed a thumb across the calluses on her fingertips, sore from playing her cello for two hours straight. "I just hope the check doesn't bounce."

She snapped her jaw shut. She must be more tired than she thought. That was a bit much, even from her.

Caitlin poked her shoulder from behind while Jazzy said, "Don't be such a sourpuss. Of course the check won't bounce."

Liz half turned to give Caitlin a crooked grin. Good thing her friend knew her well enough to see through her cynicism and realize the reason for her grumpiness.

The car slowed as they approached the entrance to Liz's apartment complex.

"I thought we played well. Did you notice—"

"What's going on over there?" Jazzy cut her off with a finger stabbing at the windshield.

Liz looked where Jazzy had indicated. Flashing blue and white lights from a pair—no, three police cars sliced through the dark haze of the downpour.

"They look like they're in front of your building, Liz."

Liz leaned forward to peer through the torrent of rain as Jazzy guided the car through the parking lot. As they drew near, a person in a dark rain poncho exited her building and sloshed through the water pooling on the sidewalk. The figure slid inside one of the police cars. Oh, no. What if something had happened to one of her neighbors?

What she noticed next made her stomach twist. A light shone in the second floor window on the left side of the building.

Her window.

She had turned off the lights before she left. She always did.

"I think…" Her voice came out choked. She swallowed and tried again. "I think they're in my apartment."

Caitlin's gasp was almost drowned out by the rumble of thunder outside.

Jazzy pulled the car to a stop behind the third police cruiser and cut the engine. The sound of rain hammering against the roof grew louder in the silence. Dread gathered in Liz's core. Had her place been broken into? Had she been robbed?

Shuffling sounds from the backseat made Liz look around. Caitlin had pulled her hood up over her head and was tying it in place beneath her chin.

Liz cleared her throat. "You don't have to get out in this weather. You'll get soaked."

Jazzy slipped her car keys into the pocket of her raincoat before turning a disbelieving stare in Liz's direction. "Are you crazy? We're your friends. We're coming with you."

A flash of relief loosened her tense shoulders, but only for a second. She needed to get in there and see what was going on in her apartment. She braced herself, pushed open the car door and exited the vehicle at a run. Dimly aware that Jazzy and Caitlin followed, she splashed across the sidewalk and into the breezeway of her building. Water plastered her bangs to her forehead and dripped into her eyes. Blinking furiously to clear them, she ascended the six stairs in two leaps. Her friends right behind her, she skidded to a halt in front of her door.

It stood open.

Just inside the doorway, two police officers, one male, one female, blocked her way. Both wore thick rain ponchos and hats covered in plastic.

Someone rushed up beside her, and Liz felt her arm caught in a tight grip.

"Oh, Liz, I'm so sorry." Her neighbor, Mrs. Evans, peered up at her from beneath a creased brow. "You've been burgled."

No. Not again. "I have?"

Mrs. Evans nodded. "They left your door open, and I peeked in. When I saw the mess, I knew something was wrong so I called the police." Her clutch eased and she patted Liz's arm. "You're not nearly as messy as all that."

All *what?*

"You're Elizabeth Carmichael?" The female officer's badge read R. Lawrence. She and the man stood shoulder-to-shoulder so Liz couldn't see past them.

Almost fearfully, she nodded.

"I'm afraid someone made quite a mess of your apartment."

"What…" Liz cleared her throat "…what did they take?"

The other officer, T. Franklin, lifted a shoulder. "You're going to have to tell us." He stepped aside and gestured for Liz to enter.

She took a step forward and stopped. A shudder ran down her spine. The sight that greeted her was hauntingly familiar.

The couch cushions had been pulled off and tossed aside. Books lay strewn over the floor in front of the empty bookcase. Sheet music littered the floor.

"Oh, no," said Caitlin behind her.

"Not again." Jazzy's whisper echoed her thoughts.

Liz's hand rose involuntarily to her throat. Once before she and her friends had been the victim of a break-in when their trio was hired to play at an out-of-town wedding. Only, then she'd been present when the intruder arrived.

But that was four months ago. That man was in prison for murder.

"As far as we can see," Officer Franklin said, "your television and stereo are here, and your computer is in the other room. We need you to walk through, and without touching anything, tell us if you notice anything missing."

"The bedroom looks worse." Liz winced at Officer Lawrence's sympathetic warning.

While Jazzy, Caitlin and Mrs. Evans waited by the door, Liz stepped slowly across the living room. Hands clasped to keep from picking anything up, she did a mental inventory. CDs and DVDs were scattered around the floor. Were any missing? Impossible to tell. Sheet music…well, she wouldn't know until she went through it, but she couldn't imagine anyone would want her cello music. Her DVD player had been pushed cockeyed, but it was still there. Still showed the correct time, even.

Bracing herself, she headed for the bedroom. The officers followed. Bile churned in her stomach when she saw the mess the intruder had left: dresser drawers upended all over the floor; the mattress shoved off the box springs; the contents of her jewelry box scattered across the top of the dresser.

Her computer desk drawers had been dumped and her personal papers strewn everywhere. Bank statements, receipts, letters, all littered the room. Hard to tell if any were missing. She'd have to alert the bank and her credit card companies, just in case they'd taken something, or made note of her account numbers. But the computer was still there.

"Do you have any firearms that may be missing, Miss Carmichael?"

Liz whirled toward Officer Franklin. "No. Nothing like that."

"How about the jewelry?" asked Officer Lawrence. "Is it all there?"

Liz's fingers hovered over the brooch on her blouse as she inspected the tangle of necklaces, earrings and bracelets. She didn't wear much jewelry, and didn't own any expensive pieces. A couple of pieces from her grandmother had sentimental value, but there was certainly nothing a thief would want.

"I don't understand." She looked at the officers. "There doesn't seem to be anything missing."

"Well, count yourself lucky." Officer Franklin's smile flashed on and off again. He turned on his heel and headed back toward the living room.

Looking at the disaster all around her, Liz didn't feel very lucky.

Officer Lawrence offered a more genuine smile. "It might have been kids looking for cash. We'll dust for prints and see if we can find anything. In the meantime, here's my card. If you discover anything missing, you be sure to let us know, okay?"

Throat tight, Liz nodded. She followed the woman back into the living room, where her friends rushed forward to enfold her in a group hug.

"You don't have to stay here," Caitlin whispered. "You can come home with me tonight."

Jazzy's head nodded against hers. "Tomorrow we'll come back and help you clean up. And we'll get new locks for your door and windows."

Liz returned the pressure of their embrace. She had never been more grateful for her friends.

From his vantage point on the other side of the parking lot, Jason slumped low behind the steering wheel and watched the shadowy figures moving back and forth through the window. Dark sheets of rain shrouded his car and protected him from the cops' sight.

He fingered his cell phone. Duke wasn't gonna like this. But putting off the call only postponed the inevitable. He dialed the number.

The call was answered on the second ring. "Did you get it?"

"It wasn't there."

The sound of soft swearing greeted his news.

"You're sure you aren't mistaken."

Jason's teeth snapped together at the implication that he couldn't handle a simple job. When he could reply in an even tone, he said, "I'm sure. I know everything that girl has in her apartment. It ain't there."

The silence on the line went on longer than Jason's patience. "You want me to nab her?"

"No."

The answer was quick, too quick. Was Duke thinking about taking him off the job? Jason couldn't afford that. His take on this job was gonna pay off some pressing gambling debts.

"It won't be like before." He gulped, remembering Duke's blistering tirade when he'd roughed up an old guy last week. Duke had been furious with Jason, but who knew the guy would come home early and catch him? At least he got the goods, and was well away before the cops arrived. "Let me talk to her nice. I'll bump into her in a restaurant or something, pour on the charm. I'll get it out of her."

"I don't want to risk you being seen. Again." The last word dripped derision. "Besides, I don't think that will be necessary. Our friend says he can get Miss Carmichael out here, and he's confident she'll bring it with her."

"But that'll take months." Jason did whine then. He needed money now. "I'm sure I can—"

"Don't do another thing. You just get yourself on a plane."

"The job's still mine, though, right? You ain't gonna take me off of it after I put in so much time?"

The low chuckle could have been insulting, or it could have been meant to comfort him. Jason gnawed his lower lip. He didn't want to tick the guy off.

"Don't worry, my friend. I've got several little tasks lined up to keep you busy until Miss Carmichael gets here. Just come home."

The line went quiet.

Jason straightened in the seat and reached for the ignition. As he started the rental car's engine, a shadow walked across the apartment window. Too unclear to identify, but it could have been her. He shifted into Drive, and when the car started to roll forward, he touched a finger to his forehead in a farewell gesture.

"I'll be seeing you, girlie."

TWO

"What are you doing on your day off tomorrow?"

Deputy Tim Richards picked up his Coke and took a pull on the straw before he answered. "Skiing with the wedding party."

"Oh, yeah, I remember." His lunch buddy, Deputy Adam Goins, unwrapped a cheeseburger as he answered. "This weekend's the wedding thing."

"Uh-huh. The others are out on the slopes right now without me, in fact." Tim glanced through the fast-food restaurant's windows. High above their cruisers, an American flag flapped wildly in a strong breeze. The vivid colors stood out starkly against a totally white sky that held the promise of powder soon to come. In fact, a few wind-whipped flakes were already stabbing at the glass. "That's all right. I wouldn't want to be out there today, but tomorrow's going to be great."

Adam's silent laugh shook his shoulders. "You sound like me. If there isn't a clear blue sky, no wind and at least six inches of fresh powder, I'd rather stay home. I'm not surprised you've become a snow snob, now that you've been in Park City a while. You've lived here three years, right?"

"Right. But I've lived in Utah all my life."

Born and raised not forty minutes from here, Tim hadn't even left his hometown for college. He'd attended the University of Utah, down in the Salt Lake valley, and roomed with his childhood friend, Ryan, the groom-to-be.

"Yeah, you know what I'm talking about. So you're off until, when? Monday?"

"Sunday. The wedding's Saturday night."

Tim bit into a couple of fries. Ryan and Debbie had decided to get married up here in Park City, instead of down in Salt Lake where they lived. Some romantic idea of Debbie's, probably, to get married at a ski lodge. Tim figured it must be costing Debbie's family a bundle. Nothing in Park City came cheap.

Of course, they were probably getting the musicians for free.

He took another drink from the straw, but his throat felt suddenly clogged. It wasn't the fries. It was the thought of the musicians. Or rather, one musician.

Liz would arrive late tonight. After three long years, he would see her tomorrow.

If he choked on the mere thought of her now, how would he act when he actually saw her?

Snow swirled around Jason as he glided down the slope. The place was practically deserted. The lifts would stop running at four, in ten more minutes. Most everybody had already headed down the mountain toward the lodge. Big flakes slapped at his goggles and gathered in the creases on the front of his ski suit. He could barely make out the trees on the other side of the run. A miserable day to be out on the slopes, but he had a meeting to attend. One he couldn't miss.

He glanced backward to make sure nobody was coming around on his left, then zipped into the thick evergreens lining the west side of the slope. The wind wasn't nearly as bad here, and he was shielded from the worst of the heavily falling snow. Weird place to hold a meeting, if you asked him. But nobody did. Just told him where to be and when to be there. Jason made it a practice to do as he was told.

A snowboarder in a dark jacket waited at the appointed spot, one foot planted in the soft snow and the other still attached to the binding of his board. Jason glided to a stop nearby. At first he thought it might be Duke, but when the guy pushed his goggles up on his hat, he realized it was someone new. Jason's pulse kicked up a notch or two. Was he finally going to meet Duke's mysterious boss?

"Hey, how's it going?" The man clipped his words short.

Jason replied with a guarded nod. "Some day out there, huh?"

A sound from behind made him turn in time to see a skier zigzag through the trees toward them. Jason admired the way the man maneuvered in the close area, the precision with which the edges of his skis carved through the deep snow. He zoomed up to them, planted his ski poles and raised his goggles like the first guy.

About time Duke got here.

"I see you two have met." Cold blue eyes slid from Jason toward the stranger.

"Not proper like. I didn't catch your name." Jason kept his tone deferential, just in case.

The man stiffened, and his eyelids narrowed.

Duke pulled off his knit hat and slapped it against his thigh. Dislodged snow flew through the air. "I don't think names will be necessary."

Jason had taken off his glove, ready to thrust his hand toward the man by way of introduction. Instead, he shoved it back on and grabbed the handle of his pole.

"I don't have long." The stranger pulled back the cinched wristband of his jacket to look at his watch. "They're going to wonder where I've gone. So say whatever you brought me here to say and let's go before we're spotted."

Jason studied the man with interest. So Duke had invited him to the meeting, not the other way around. He wasn't the boss, then. Duke had mentioned another guy who was in on this job, a new guy. Someone who insisted he could get the Carmichael chick out to Utah.

Duke pulled the hat back on and settled it over his ears. "I just wanted to touch base with you both. Make sure we all understand the plan."

"I don't need to understand any plan. I've done my part."

Jason dipped his head to look at the snow between his ski tips. This guy had nerve, he'd give him that. Jason wouldn't dare talk to Duke in that tone.

But when he risked an upward glance, he saw that Duke's face remained impassive. "She arrives tonight?"

The man nodded. "As arranged."

"And you're sure she'll have it with her?"

The other man gave an impatient grunt. "I don't see why I have to repeat myself. I've assured you she'll have it."

A flash of indignation set Jason's teeth against each other. The guy's tone spoke volumes about the relationship between these two. The newcomer sounded like a man talking to his partner. Duke apparently accepted him as such, while he kept Jason at arm's length, handing out orders with no explanation and expecting unquestioning obedience. Like Jason was some kind of flunky or something.

Duke smiled. "Good. I think that's all we need from you, then. You can go."

Disgust curled one corner of the man's mouth. "You brought me out here for that?"

"Unless you'd like to stay and hear the rest of the plan. I'm sure we can find another part for you to play. I rather thought you preferred not to dirty your hands with the details, though."

Jason had a hard time keeping a straight face at the speed

with which the guy snapped his goggles over his eyes and zipped away, pushing his board across the snow with his unbound boot. Within seconds he was lost from view in the blinding snow beyond the mass of trees.

A gust of wind whistled through the pine needles and rattled the branches above them. A mound of snow fell on Jason's skis. He used the tip of his pole to scrape it off.

"So my part of the plan," he said, "is to go through her room tomorrow when she leaves. You got a passkey for me?"

"I have a passkey." Duke pulled the glove off his right hand and shoved it under his left arm. "And I have something else, another little thing to take care of."

Jason stabbed the pole into the soft snow. Duke always had a "little thing" he wanted Jason to take care of. Next thing you knew, Duke would be ordering Jason to pick up his dry cleaning or something.

"Okay, but I'm upping my price this time." Emboldened by the stranger's tone with Duke, Jason spoke more forcefully than he would have before. "All these things I've been doing for you—running down to Vegas or over to Denver to pick up packages—they take a lot of time. More than I thought. And besides, you never tell me what I'm doing. I'm starting to think you don't trust me or something."

Duke unzipped his ski suit. The cold smile on his thin lips sent a shiver through Jason that had nothing to do with temperature.

"Actually, you're right," Duke replied. "I don't trust you. You're sloppy, and since I've developed a relationship with some new associates in Europe, I can't afford to surround myself with sloppiness."

He reached into the breast of his ski suit. When he pulled his hand out, Jason went completely still. Duke held a pistol with a silencer attached. And it was pointed directly at Jason's forehead.

THREE

The snow on the ski slope outside Liz Carmichael's balcony glowed in the pale moonlight. Tall fir trees tossed long shadows across the frozen surface of the smooth trail as far up the mountain as she could see. Branches gyrated in an icy gust of wind and the shadows danced on the snow. Then a heavy cloud raced across the sky, blotting out the moonlight and hiding the stars from view.

Liz shuddered as the icy breeze reached her balcony. The wind here had a different quality than in Kentucky, probably because the frigid Utah air didn't hold a trace of Kentucky's trademark humidity. At least the climate made the snow light and powdery, great for skiing, something she didn't get the chance to do back home.

Back home. That was the first time she could remember thinking of Kentucky as home. She leaned her elbows on the balcony railing and bent to rest her chin in her hands as her gaze wandered up the mountainside. But where else would she call "home" if not Kentucky? Not Portland, where Mom and Dad lived and where she had grown up. Too much time had passed since she'd left. Mom and Dad lived in a condo now, and she felt like a visitor when she went to stay with them at Christmas. That old saying was true, you can't go home again.

There was a time in college when Utah had started to feel like home, but that was in the past, and had been for three years.

Until now. Because the part of her past she most dreaded seeing lived here. Was nearby even now, somewhere in this trendy resort town. A familiar guilt stabbed at her, and her thoughts skittered away from memories of the incident so fresh in her mind it might have happened yesterday.

The cloud moved past the moon, and white light illuminated the landscape as a movement down below on the slope caught her eye. A bulky figure carrying a long snowboard tromped through the darkness toward the chairlift on the other side of the thick tree line. Liz glanced at her watch. After 1:00 a.m. Strange time to hike up for a ride. Maybe a treasure hunter.

Locals did that sometimes, combing the slopes after hours looking for valuables dropped from the chairlift. Not usually at 1:00 a.m., though. Maybe it was a snowboarder who had lost something on the slopes during the day and couldn't sleep until he found it.

The glass door behind her slid open. She didn't straighten from her position leaning across the railing, but turned her head to identify Caitlin stepping through the door.

"Brrrr." Her friend rubbed her arms briskly beneath a pink terry cloth bathrobe. "What are you doing out here? It's freezing."

"Couldn't sleep."

Caitlin stepped up beside her. "Me either. A long travel day always does that to me. Jazzy doesn't seem to have the same problem, though. She's completely zonked out."

Liz glanced backward through the glass and toward the closed bedroom door of the condo. "When did she finally hang up?" The third member of their trio had been on the phone with her boyfriend since the plane's wheels touched the landing strip at the Salt Lake International Airport.

"About thirty minutes ago." Caitlin laughed. "Isn't it great to see how happy she is with Derrick?"

Liz bit back a snarky response. "Great" wasn't how she would describe Jazzy's obsession with her new boyfriend. "Nauseating" was the word she'd use.

But she was trying hard to control her tongue on this trip, so she remained silent.

"Are you sure nothing else is bothering you? You've been really quiet since we got here. That's not like you."

There *was* something bothering her. Nerves had twisted her stomach to knots as she'd walked through the airport, watching for a familiar face to materialize in the crowd at any minute. She'd stared at every tall, dark-haired guy they passed, daring one of them to show up, and half-afraid they both would. When she was finally seated in the rental car with her friends, their instrument cases and luggage piled in the trunk and the backseat, she'd realized neither of them was coming. But instead of relief, the knots had tightened even further. Why couldn't one of them have met her at the airport? Then she could have put the dread of those first meetings behind her.

Caitlin was watching her closely. Liz gave a half smile. "I'm a little uptight. Can't stop thinking about all the family stuff I'm going to have to deal with tomorrow."

Her friend's eyebrows formed surprised arches. "Have you seen your relatives at all since you left college?"

Liz shook her head. "Only Mom and Dad. None of the Utah contingent. And my grandma's going to let me hear about it, too."

"Well, your cousin's wedding is a perfect opportunity for a reunion." Caitlin linked an arm through hers. "Come on inside. You don't want to get sick."

There's an idea. If she was sick, she'd have the perfect excuse to miss all the wedding festivities. And all the wedding guests. Especially the best man.

With a sigh, Liz straightened. She was healthy as a horse, and she wasn't going to fake an illness. Debbie was her favorite cousin. They'd been as close as sisters growing up. After Debbie's mother died, she'd spent every summer with Liz and her family.

Since Debbie had paid for Liz and her friends to fly all the way to Utah to play at her wedding—or more likely, spent hours convincing Grandma to pay for their trip—the least Liz could do was show up and look happy.

As she turned, the chairlift on the other side of the tree line started to move. Ah, that explained the middle-of-the-night stroll. It was an employee doing some sort of facility check or something. Weird timing but she'd noticed a line of groomers leveling the snow up on the mountain when they arrived, and it was ten o'clock then. The resort must have to do a lot of their maintenance work after hours, when the skiers were asleep.

Caitlin slid the glass door open and gestured for Liz to precede her. "You're going to have a great time this weekend, Liz. Not only do you get to enjoy a reunion with your family, but you're bound to see some of your college friends, too."

Liz stepped into the warmth of the suite. Yes, some of her friends from college were in the wedding party. And at least one person she would not categorize as a friend. A handsome face swam into focus in her mind. Her heart heaved with a guilty thud. Suddenly, three years didn't seem very long. Not nearly long enough.

FOUR

Despite the late hour when she finally fell asleep, Liz's body refused to conform to the two-hour time difference between Kentucky and Utah. Her eyes popped open at six o'clock in the morning.

"Nooo!" She turned over in the bed and covered her head with a pillow to block the sight of the despicable red numbers glaring at her from the alarm clock. Four hours' sleep was definitely not enough, not with the busy day in store for her.

But a return to sleep proved impossible. Her body told her it was after eight, high time to be up and about. With a resigned sigh, she heaved herself out of bed and stumbled, bleary-eyed, to the bathroom for a shower.

Thirty minutes later, dressed and as ready to face the day as she would ever be, Liz headed for the kitchen of the two-bedroom condo Cousin Debbie reserved for them. The place wasn't fancy, but diehard skiers typically didn't care, as long as they had a bed and someplace to dry out their ski clothes at night. The furnishings in the sitting area, an attractive sofa and love seat combo, were clean enough to satisfy even the fastidious Jazzy. The coffee table boasted a few small dings and dents, but the dust-free surface gleamed, and the lemony scent of polish lingering in the air spoke well of the house-keeper's attention to detail.

The door to the second bedroom was closed. Jazzy and Caitlin were apparently still sleeping.

At least some of us will be rested today, the lucky dogs.

Liz searched the cabinets in the compact kitchen. A set of dishes—two sizes of plates, cereal bowls, mugs with saucers— lay neatly stacked in one, and an assortment of glasses in another. The rest of the cabinets were empty. A coffeemaker sat on the counter, taunting her with its empty carafe.

Wish I'd remembered to pack some coffee. We're going to the grocery today no matter what.

Liz grabbed her purse and headed for the lobby.

Though the town of Park City boasted many timeshares, condos and hotels, the lodge at Eagle Summit was situated adjacent to the main chairlift of the small, privately-owned ski resort. Out-of-town skiers loved being able to walk a mere hundred feet from their condos to the lift. And a city bus stopped right in front of the lodge, if guests chose to ski at the bigger and more famous area resorts, Deer Valley and Park City Mountain Resort.

Liz preferred Eagle Summit. During her years in college, she'd skied here fairly often. Eagle Summit had fewer chair- lifts and not as much in the way of vertical terrain as the more well-known resorts, but Liz had always enjoyed the wide, tree-lined slopes that management kept meticulously groomed. And the lower price college kids paid for a day pass counted for a lot.

Liz remembered one time when she and Tim were skiing—

She skidded to a halt on the stone-tiled floor as she entered the lobby area. *No! I will not take a stroll down Memory Lane!*

Being back in Utah, and especially up in Park City where Liz had spent so much time with Tim, would trigger a lot of memories if she allowed her mind to wander in that direction. Which she did *not* intend to do.

In the lobby a dark-haired woman sat behind the front desk, a highly polished counter to the right of the main entryway. She looked up when Liz entered, nodded, and went back to whatever she was doing. Liz scanned the lobby. *Wouldn't you think they'd have coffee set up for the guests who don't want to fix their own up in their rooms?* She couldn't see any, though.

Beyond the front desk was a coffee shop with no sign of movement in the darkened interior. A copy of today's edition of *USA TODAY* rested on the floor in front of the glass door. She spotted a small sign that said they'd open at seven. A wave of irritation tightened her lips, but she forced herself to relax. She'd been up for almost an hour already without coffee; another ten minutes wouldn't hurt her.

She wandered in the direction of a huge stone fireplace in a cozy sitting area that took up one corner of the lobby. Over-stuffed chairs and a big, comfy-looking sofa were clustered around a furry bearskin rug, while a giant moose head stared mournfully at her from above a rough wooden mantle. Though dead animals wouldn't be Liz's first choice of room décor, in a lodge-type setting, with thick cedar beams criss-crossing the high ceiling, it worked. She crossed to stand in front of the hearth, enjoying the heat still emanating from a few ash-covered embers in the grate. To the left of the fire-place, three floor-to-ceiling windows looked out onto the deserted slopes. The morning sun was starting to lighten the sky but had not yet managed to climb above the mountain peaks. Deep shadows covered the snow-packed ski area.

A jingle behind her made her turn. A fiftyish man dressed in a dark gray suit strode across the lobby fingering a huge set of keys and mumbling to himself. He approached the coffee shop, picked up the newspaper and fitted a key into the lock, his lips moving as he muttered.

Finally. Maybe a jolt of caffeine would chase the heavy

tiredness out of her limbs. Liz followed the man through the door.

"Oh." He turned a startled look her way, which he immediately replaced with a professional smile. "Good morning. I'll bet you're looking for a cup of coffee."

Well, duh. That's why I'm in a coffee shop. But Liz returned his smile and managed a pleasant, "I sure am."

"It'll take me a minute to get it started. The girl who was supposed to open this morning just called in sick, so I've got to…" He disappeared into a room behind the serving counter. The drone of his voice continued, though Liz couldn't make out the words. The overhead lights flickered on, brightening the room considerably. A second later he reappeared, a foil packet in each hand. "But at least you know it'll be fresh." He held the packets up for her inspection. "Regular or decaf?"

Liz didn't hesitate. "Definitely regular."

"Coming right up." He whirled around to a metal commercial coffee machine on the back counter and pulled an oversize filter off a stack on a shelf above it. "I haven't seen you before. Have you been at Eagle Summit all week?"

Liz paced to the far end of the counter to peek into a glass display case. Parchment-covered trays lined two shelves, empty except for a couple of bran muffins. Her stomach threatened to rumble, but there was no telling how long those muffins had been there.

"No, my friends and I arrived last night."

He slid the basket of coffee grounds into place and pressed a button. The high-pitched sound of water running through pipes began as he turned toward her and extended a hand across the counter. "I didn't think I'd seen you before. I'm Greg Harrison. My wife and I own the place."

Surprised, Liz shook his hand. "You own the lodge?"

He waved toward the back wall, beyond which lay the ski area base. "And the resort. Well, us and the bank, of course.

We bought it a couple of years ago." He glanced at the muffins in the case. "Oh, don't even think about eating those. The bakery should be here with their daily delivery any minute."

Liz slid into one of the tall wooden chairs as he pulled the old muffins out and wadded up the crumb-covered parchment paper. Eagle Summit must be a smaller business than she thought, if the owner had to step in when a coffee shop worker called in sick.

He chatted as he wiped the trays down and lined them with fresh paper. "My wife oversees the ski resort, and since my background is in the hospitality industry, I take care of the lodge."

"You both must stay pretty busy."

"You know it." He flashed a grin in her direction as he slid an empty tray back into the case. "But at least we love what we're doing." He raised a hand and snapped his fingers in the air. "You're with the Carmichael wedding party!"

"That's right. How did you know?"

He grimaced. "I wish I could say we have so many reservations that it's hard to keep track of all the guests, but that wouldn't be true. We've been looking forward to this wedding for months. Besides, you look like you're related to the bride."

"She's my cousin."

His smile brightened. "Ah, then you're the musician from Tennessee."

"Kentucky, but yes."

"I'm eager to hear what you think of our new reception room. I hope the acoustics are okay. Your cousin's is the first wedding we've held in it since we remodeled."

"I'm sure it will be fine."

He flashed an absent smile in her direction and went into the back room again. The odor of fresh coffee permeated the air and Liz watched the carafe fill with the dark liquid.

Mr. Harrison returned with a pitcher of cream and a con-

tainer full of sweetener packets just as the stream of coffee
slowed to a drip.

"There you go." He set an oversize mug on the counter in
front of her. "Those fresh muffins should be here any minute."

Liz sipped her coffee black from the mug. *Ah!*

"It's okay," she assured him. "I'm meeting the bride for
breakfast at eight." She lifted the mug in a mock salute. "This
is perfect until then."

She picked up her mug with one hand and retrieved the
newspaper from where he'd tossed it on the counter, then
selected one of the six tables lining the wall. The chairs were
spindly and narrow, a fifties diner–type look with red vinyl
seat cushions. Liz indulged in a broad smile as she imagined
Grandma's reaction to their insufficient width when she
arrived in…she glanced at her watch…about forty minutes.

The bedroom walls were closing in on Tim. For the mil-
lionth time he glanced at the clock on the nightstand. Six
minutes since the last time he checked. Twenty-seven minutes
since the time before. And one hundred eighty-four minutes
since he first woke at 3:07 a.m. with his brain whirling around
the thought he could not banish. Liz was here, at Eagle
Summit Resort just a few minutes away. He would see her
today.

Lord, does she ever think about me?

Dread and anticipation churned together in his gut. How
would she react when she saw him?

With a jerk, he threw off the blanket and rolled out of bed.
His mind had become his enemy, this room his prison. He had
to get up, get moving. A hot shower would do him a world
of good, clear his head.

He flipped the wall switch and light flooded his sparsely
furnished bedroom. Two steps took him to his dresser,
where he gathered his clothes. As he slid the drawer shut,

his gaze fell on a small black box nestled amid the odds and ends on the surface of his dresser. What perverse sense of self-punishment stopped him from getting rid of the thing three years ago, like he should have? He'd started to a dozen times. As long as he kept it where he could take it out and look at it every so often, moving on was impossible. But something always held him back.

Swallowing hard, he picked up the box and hesitantly opened the lid. The diamond caught the light and winked at him from its bed of black velvet.

Maybe this weekend he could finally get some closure, put the past behind him.

Tim snapped the box closed and held it for a moment in his hand. Then he set it back on the dresser.

Two refills later, when she had read every interesting article in the paper and had just started on the sports section out of desperation, a familiar figure finally stepped through the doorway.

"Liz! I'm so glad to see you!"

Liz stood as Debbie raced across the room to gather her in a hug. Liz returned the embrace with as much enthusiasm as the bride-to-be. It had been far too long since she'd seen Debbie. Though they'd been in constant touch through e-mail, she realized with a sudden rush of emotion just how much she'd missed her cousin and college roommate—far more than she had allowed herself to realize.

Her hands lingered on Debbie's arms after their fierce embrace ended, and she looked her cousin over. Debbie was largely unchanged. If anything, she was prettier than ever, with her thick, dark hair falling well past her shoulders, and bangs accenting her round eyes.

"You look fantastic," Debbie said at the same time Liz gushed, "You're going to be a beautiful bride!"

Their laughter mingled, and three years melted away.

"Ahem!"

An indignant voice cut into their reunion. Liz, her back to the new arrival, took a deep breath and rolled her eyes at Debbie, who bit back a giggle. Steeling her expression, Liz turned to face the third-most-dreaded encounter of the weekend.

"Grandma, you look wonderful." She knew her voice gushed, but she couldn't stop herself. "You haven't aged a day."

Actually, she hadn't. Her grandmother looked exactly the same as she had three years ago. Finger curls of steel-gray hair still clung tightly to her scalp. The same knowing, brown gaze pierced Liz like a laser beam. And the floral-print dress she wore, not to mention the support hose and sturdy black shoes, were as familiar as Liz's own wardrobe. Only a lot older.

"Elizabeth. I'm glad you decided to show up. I half-expected you wouldn't."

Yeah. Same Grandma.

The old lady accepted a kiss of greeting, then pulled out a chair and examined the small cushion with a jaundiced eye. Liz hid a smile as Grandma pushed the chair back under the table and turned toward Mr. Harrison, who hovered behind the counter, watching their reunion.

"I believe we'll take our coffee out on the sofa in the lobby. Can you send someone to build up the fire?"

"Of course, Mrs. Carmichael. I'll bring a tray out immediately." His tone was deferential. Apparently Mr. Harrison had encountered Grandma before this morning.

Debbie linked arms with Liz as they followed Grandma to the lobby. "How was your flight? Everything okay with your room?"

"The flight was uneventful," Liz told her, "and the room is great."

She'd barely settled in a square, overstuffed chair catty-corner to the couch that Grandma claimed when Mr. Harrison arrived with a tray full of coffee and Danish. He set it on the rough-hewn sofa table and filled two mugs from the carafe, then refilled Liz's, as well. With a slight bow toward Grandma and a grin in Liz's direction, he disappeared silently.

Grandma stirred three sugar packets into her coffee, raised her mug to her lips and caught Liz's gaze over the rim. "Elizabeth, I hope you've brought *it*."

There was no need to wonder what Grandma referred to. Liz gulped a fortifying sip of scalding coffee.

"There you are!"

She turned gratefully toward the timely interruption. Jazzy and Caitlin strode across the lobby, looking much brighter and more alert than Liz felt. Liz inspected her friends with fresh eyes, aware that Grandma was examining them through her usual critical lens.

Liz performed the introductions. "Grandma and Debbie, these are my friends from Kentucky. Jazzy plays the violin, and Caitlin the flute."

Astute about the niceties with elderly relatives, they each shook hands with Grandma first, and then the bride. Petite Jazzy turned on her elfin grin. "Mrs. Carmichael, I'm so pleased to meet you. Liz has spoken of you."

Grandma sent a suspicious glance at Liz. "Has she now?"

Jazzy nodded and settled into the chair opposite Liz as Caitlin eyed the tray. "I'm going to go grab some coffee. Want some, Jazz?"

"Please."

"Would you see if they have any butter for these rolls, dear?" Grandma gave Caitlin a brief smile. "Not that I expect them to have real butter, but it doesn't hurt to ask."

"Yes, ma'am."

While Caitlin headed toward the coffee shop, Grandma

turned a hard stare toward Liz. "As I was saying, Elizabeth. Have you brought it?"

A cold shaft shot through Liz. She felt like a kid again, pinned under Grandma's glare. She nodded.

Grandma's eyebrows arched. "Well?"

Aware of Jazzy's curious stare and Debbie's cringe, Liz reached for her purse, which she'd placed on the floor beside the chair. Under the watchful gaze of Grandma, she fished in the depths of the leather bag until her fingers encountered a familiar silken box. She pulled it out and, cradling the box in her hand, flipped the lid open.

Inside, a golden, jeweled brooch, shaped like a dragonfly, nestled against a red velvet background. Delicate pearls and glittering emeralds, undoubtedly fake but still beautiful, caught the dull lobby lights and tossed rainbow glints toward her. She took a long, last look at the pin, bidding it a mental farewell, then snapped the lid closed and held it toward Grandma.

"Here you are."

Grandma drew both hands up to her chest and reared backward, her expression horrified. "I can't take it back! It has passed on, however inappropriately. Give it to her."

She nodded toward Debbie.

Liz extended the box toward her cousin. Debbie's eyes widened, creases wrinkling her smooth brow. Her hands remained clasped in her lap.

"I don't know, Grandma," she said, her gaze on the box. "Seems to me like it should wait until after the wedding. Don't you think?"

"Not *after* the wedding, dear." Grandma's lipsticked mouth pursed. "But it's true that my mother gave it to me on my wedding day, not before." Her glare caught Liz's gaze and held it. "Perhaps it is safer to wait until the day of the wedding. We don't want to repeat the dreadful mistakes of the past."

A rush of heat ran from the top of Liz's head through her core. No, of course she didn't want a repeat performance of what had happened to her and Tim. Still, if a mistake had been made, it could only be attributed to Grandma, the person who had jumped the gun in passing down the heirloom brooch. But Liz certainly wasn't going to point that out.

"Liz?" Jazzy leaned forward in her chair, her face full of questions. "You're giving away your pin? But you love that pin."

Caitlin arrived in time to hear Jazzy's question, and turned an inquiring gaze on Liz as she handed Jazzy a full coffee mug.

"Love it or not," Grandma said, her voice unyielding, "it is not hers to keep. It belongs to Deborah now."

"Not yet," Debbie rushed to say. "Not until I'm married." The smile she turned toward Liz held a touch of desperation. "It's yours for another three days."

Liz drew her hand back to her lap and curled her fingers protectively around the box. The silk felt cool and smooth to her touch.

"I don't understand." Caitlin dropped onto the third sofa cushion, on the other side of Grandma. "I thought that pin was an heirloom that's been in your family for a long time."

"Oh, it has." Grandma sipped from her coffee before returning the mug to the sofa table. She settled back. "I have an oil painting of my grandmother wearing the brooch in 1885, when she first immigrated to this country from England. That would be Elizabeth and Deborah's great-great-grandmother."

"Wow." Jazzy eyed the box in Liz's hand. "So Liz got to keep it for a while, and now it goes to Debbie?"

Liz gritted her teeth. Here it came. She had been friends with these girls for three years, since she moved to Kentucky and joined the Lexington Community Church young adult group, but she'd never told them—or anyone else in Kentucky—about the shameful part of her past.

Grandma turned a highbrowed glare her way. "It would have stayed with Elizabeth if she had married that nice young man she was engaged to, like she was supposed to."

FIVE

"Engaged?" Caitlin's blond eyebrows shot upward and disappeared beneath her bangs.

Liz squirmed under her friend's openmouthed stare.

Jazzy looked as shocked as Caitlin. "You never told us you were engaged."

Liz sank lower in the chair. A lame excuse came to mind: *The subject never came up!* But now was not the time, nor the place, to get into a big discussion about her past. She gave Jazzy an "I'd rather not talk about this right now" look.

But Grandma either didn't see it or didn't care. "Oh, yes. She was engaged to a fine young man she'd dated all the way through college, a local boy from a good family. His parents go to my church." She frowned at Liz. "After Elizabeth broke his heart, I couldn't look them in the eye for months."

Liz opened her mouth to say that she didn't break his heart, but she closed it again. The expression on Tim's face that night still haunted her. To say she hadn't broken his heart would be a lie.

"Liz was right to break off the engagement," Debbie argued loyally. "Marriage is a serious step, a lifetime commitment. If she wasn't one-hundred-percent sure, she did the right thing."

Liz gave her a grateful look, but she could see the unspoken accusation hovering in her cousin's eyes.

I know, I know. I could have handled it a lot better.

"That's as it may be," Grandma said, "but it doesn't change the fact that the brooch is to pass to the first woman to marry in each generation of our family." She closed her eyes briefly and inclined her head over her mug. "Perhaps I acted hastily in giving Elizabeth the brooch as an engagement present. Since I was blessed with two sons and no daughters, I was too eager to see the heirloom handed down. I never dreamed the outcome would be so…" Her lips tightened. "Disappointing."

Time to change the subject. Liz dropped the box into her purse and straightened in her chair.

"I'll hold on to it until Saturday, then," she told Debbie. "So. What's on the agenda for today?"

Judging from the expressions on Jazzy's and Caitlin's faces, the subject was far from closed. A third degree loomed on the horizon, but at least they were willing to delay the discussion.

Debbie, too, thank goodness. "We've got about a million appointments," she said. "You are coming along with Grandma and me to visit the florist and the caterer, and I need to stop by the jewelry store sometime and pick up Ryan's ring." Her gaze shifted to Caitlin and Jazzy. "You two are welcome to come along with us today, if you like."

"Actually, we thought we'd take advantage of the location and go skiing." Caitlin grinned in Jazzy's direction. "Jazzy has never skied, so she's looking forward to giving it a try."

Liz tried not to envy her friends their day on the slopes. That sure did sound a lot more fun than running around Park City with her surly grandmother.

A commotion behind them caused Debbie to turn, and her face lit up. "There's Ryan! He and some of the guys are skiing today, too." She set her mug down and leaped up from the couch.

Liz started to twist in her chair. She hadn't seen her cousin's fiancé since she left Utah three years before.

Debbie froze. Her eyes widened and she looked down at Liz. "Oh, look." Her voice held a note of strain. "All Ryan's groomsmen are with him."

A sudden panic snatched the breath right out of Liz's throat. *All* his groomsmen? Including the best man?

Tim followed the guys through the front entrance of the lodge, their thick ski suits *shush, shush, shushing* with every step. He hung toward the back of their small group, half-wishing he'd arranged to meet up with them later at the chair-lift. But there was no sense in postponing the inevitable meeting. He was sure to run into Liz sooner or later. Might as well get it over with.

"There they are." Ryan lifted a hand to wave at Debbie, then slowed to fall in step with Tim as they crossed the lobby. "Looks like Liz is here. You okay with that?"

No. Not by a long shot. But what choice do I have?

Tim forced a casual smile. "Sure. Water under the bridge."

Ryan clapped him on the shoulder. "Thanks, dude."

As they approached the group by the fireplace, Debbie launched herself into Ryan's arms and greeted him with an enthusiastic kiss that belied the fact they saw each other several times a week. Tim watched their embrace with a sense of satisfaction. Ryan was his best friend, and one lucky guy. Every man deserved to have a woman who loved him like Debbie loved Ryan.

He ignored an un-Christian twinge of jealousy. *Every* man? Even him?

His gaze swept the group of women seated around the fire. A couple of strangers, Debbie's grandmother and—

Pain punched him in the gut. His feet stopped moving.

Liz sat in a big padded chair, holding on to a coffee mug with both hands. She was staring into her cup, her head tilted forward, so he indulged in a moment looking her over, noting the changes three years had wrought. Her hair had grown long. As he watched, she smoothed it behind a delicate ear. She looked a bit thinner, her neck more slender and elegant. Ah, but that chiseled nose hadn't changed, and neither had those soft lips he remembered so well.

Her shoulders rose as she drew in a breath, and in the next moment she looked up. Their gazes locked.

The breath whooshed out of his lungs.

She was even more stunning than he remembered.

Lord, this is not fair. Couldn't she have gotten uglier?

Two faint spots of color appeared on her cheeks and she looked away, but not before Tim saw her lips press firmly together. Her shoulders angled slightly away from the group, from him. He'd received some instruction in body language in his law enforcement training, so he recognized the meaning behind her unconscious gesture. She was distancing herself. She didn't want anything to do with him.

Tim cleared his throat. If that's the way she wanted to play it, fine. He rounded the sofa and stood on the other side of the coffee table from Liz and Debbie's grandmother.

"Mrs. Carmichael, it's a pleasure to see you again."

She gave him a warm smile and allowed him to take her hand. "It's been too long, young man. You should attend church with your parents more often."

"Oh, you know how it is when you have to work for a living. I don't get too many weekends off, and when I do, I have a church up here in Park City I've grown fond of."

Mrs. Carmichael released his hand and gestured toward the two strangers. "Allow me to introduce these lovely girls." She inclined her head. "But I'm afraid I've already forgotten their names."

The blonde seated on the couch beside the elderly lady extended a hand. "I'm Caitlin Saylor. And this is Jasmine Delaney."

He shook her hand and reached for the brunette's as Mrs. Carmichael identified them. "They're Elizabeth's musician friends from Kentucky, here to play at Deborah and Ryan's wedding. Girls, this is Tim Richards, Elizabeth's former fiancé."

The petite brunette's expression froze as her eyes flicked toward Liz. Then her smile widened artificially. "My friends call me Jazzy. It's nice to meet you, Tim."

"You, too." Thank goodness his voice sounded normal.

Mrs. Carmichael nodded at the girls. "Tim is a sheriff here in Park City."

"Deputy Sheriff," he corrected with a grin. "Welcome to Utah."

He steeled his expression and turned toward Liz then. "You're looking well, Liz."

A smile flashed onto her lips and disappeared just as quickly, though she didn't meet his eyes. "You, too, Tim."

The sound of her low voice caused Tim's heart to twist unexpectedly. He steeled himself against the assault of a million memories. Oh, the words that voice used to whisper in his ear.

Ryan came to his rescue.

"Liz, long time no see! C'mere and give me a hug."

Liz hurriedly set her mug on the table as Ryan pulled her out of the chair and into an embrace.

"Hey, come meet the guys."

Ryan performed the introductions and hands were shaken all around, while Tim stared out the window and battled a million memories the sight of Liz had unearthed.

He cleared his throat and nodded toward the window. "Hey, look. The lifts are running. Time to get our gear and hit the slopes."

Ryan glanced at his watch. "We have fifteen minutes. We're going to get first tracks this morning, guys. Ought to be some awesome powder after that storm came through yesterday afternoon."

Patrick, one of Ryan's friends from work, started to turn away, then stopped. "Hey, is Jeremy joining us again today?"

Everyone froze. Debbie bit her lip and cast a wary glance at Tim. Ryan's eyes widened. Even Mrs. Carmichael stared into her coffee, uncharacteristically silent. Though it took every ounce of control he could muster, Tim forced his face to remain completely impassive. And he did not look at Liz.

"Uh, not today," Ryan said. "I think he's working or something."

Thank You, Lord. I don't think I can handle both of them in one day.

"Then what are we waiting for? Let's get 'er done." Patrick, a newcomer to their group, obviously had no idea of the history he'd just unearthed. And as far as Tim was concerned, he didn't need to know. Like he told Ryan earlier, that was water under the bridge.

"Yeah," Tim agreed, "let's get going." He nodded toward Mrs. Carmichael and the girls, and continued to ignore Liz as he walked away.

While the guys headed for the door, Ryan pulled him aside. "Hey, dude, I hope you don't mind that Jeremy hung out with us yesterday. I wouldn't have asked him if you'd been along. You know that, right?"

Tim forced a laugh. "What is this, grade school? You can hang out with whoever you want. I'm your friend no matter what." He grinned. "Even if you do have really bad taste in choosing the rest of your friends."

Ryan clapped him on the shoulder. "Good man."

A figure ran across the courtyard beyond the big windows by the fireplace, and a moment later a teenager in full winter gear ran into the lobby. He left a trail of snow on the tiled floor from his snowboarding boots as he jogged toward the front desk. His voice, pitched high with excitement, carried across the lobby.

"Where's Mr. Harrison?"

Something in the kid's tone drew Tim's attention. He couldn't hear the reply mumbled by the woman at the desk. But the teenager's next statement carried clearly to the group by the fireplace.

"We found a frozen dead guy on the Crested Eagle lift!"

SIX

Liz sat straight up in her chair. Did that kid just say…

A memory surfaced. Last night, standing on the balcony, the figure trudging across the slopes in the moonlight. Later, the chairlift starting to move. Had she seen the man moments before he caught a lift ride to his death?

She turned in time to see the woman at the front desk point toward the coffee shop. The teenager ran across the lobby and dashed through the door.

"Did you hear that?" Debbie's round eyes swept the group around the fireplace.

"I certainly did." Grandma grabbed Debbie's hand over the back of the couch. "Deborah, we must find another location for the wedding immediately, though where we'll find someplace suitable on such short notice is beyond me. I'll call Reverend Bowers and see if he can free up the sanctuary."

Debbie shook her head, confusion creasing her forehead. "Why do we need to move the wedding?"

Grandma's nostrils flared. "You can't have a wedding on a property where a death has just occurred!"

Ryan returned to the group. Liz looked up in time to see Tim disappear into the coffee shop.

"Tim's going to see if he can help," Ryan told them. "He'll join us on the slopes after the sheriff gets here."

Startled, Liz's gaze flew to Ryan's face. "The sheriff? Why?"

Ryan shrugged. "Routine, I guess. A death at a local business probably needs an official statement or something. And somebody has to notify the next of kin and all that."

Debbie looked up into his face. "Do you think we should move the wedding?"

Ryan put an arm around her waist and squeezed. "No. This place is just what we wanted for our big day." He lowered his voice. "But I don't think we'll ski here today. I'm sure they'll have to close that lift for a while, and that will shut down all the runs it services."

Debbie looked at Jazzy. "If you're still planning on skiing today you might want to go with the guys."

"You're welcome to join us," Ryan said. "We'll probably head over to Park City Mountain."

"Sounds like a good idea," Jazzy said, and Caitlin nodded. "I've never been on skis, so I can learn there as well as here."

"Park City Mountain's ski school is really good," Debbie said. "You can sign up for a lesson when you buy your lift ticket."

The sight of that figure carrying a snowboard across the snow would not leave Liz's mind. She really didn't want to go into that coffee shop with Tim in there, but what if she was the only one who had witnessed the dead person's final moments? She stood abruptly. Everyone looked at her.

"I need to talk to Mr. Harrison," she said.

Grandma's voice followed her. "We have a schedule to keep today!"

"I'll only be a minute."

Liz stepped through the open doorway in time to hear the end of the teenager's account. Tim glanced at her once, then returned his attention to the kid. Thank goodness. Even that brief glance made her want to scurry for cover, like a bug on the kitchen floor. She had forgotten how handsome he was.

Or maybe she'd just *wanted* to forget. Either way, she certainly hadn't anticipated feeling a surge of attraction when she saw him again, and she didn't like it. Not one bit.

"…and Cameron said he thought it was a joke, you know? Like the time Dawson dressed up his mom's sewing dummy in ski clothes and sent it up the lift. But when Cameron tried to pull it off, he saw it wasn't no dummy." The kid's eyes went round. "It was a dead guy."

Mr. Harrison emitted a strangled moan.

"Where is the body now?" Tim's voice held an authoritative note that Liz had never heard. Of course, he had become a deputy after she moved to Kentucky, so she'd never seen him in an official capacity. His steady tone acted as a calming counterpoint to the teenager's shrill delivery.

"Up at the top of the lift, lying on the unloading ramp. It fell off the chair when Cameron jerked it." He included Liz in his explanation. A patch of stark white skin surrounded his eyes like a mask on his deeply tanned face, caused by hours in the sun wearing ski goggles. He looked back at Mr. Harrison. "He called the base, and Mrs. Harrison sent the ski patrol over there. Then she told me to come tell you, because you didn't answer your cell phone."

"It's back in my office." Mr. Harrison's expression became apprehensive. "Did Cameron say who it was?"

The teen shrugged. "He didn't say."

Tim unzipped the breast pocket of his ski suit and pulled out a cell phone. "I'll call the sheriff."

The resort owner started visibly, then gave a resigned nod. "Thank you, Brandon. Tell Mrs. Harrison we'll need a couple of snowmobiles when the sheriff arrives."

Brandon nodded and left, leaving Liz alone with Mr. Harrison…and Tim. He spoke into his phone in curt, clipped sentences. Mr. Harrison watched from his position on the other side of the counter, while Liz stood next to Tim, so close she could smell the subtle scent of his aftershave. He was still wearing the same brand he'd worn in college. She took a sideways step, putting a comfortable distance between her and her ex-fiancé.

Tim disconnected the call and dropped it back into his pocket. Only then did he finally look at her, his expression politely blank. "Did you need something?"

"I—" Liz cleared her throat. "I might have seen something. Last night. Uh, I mean this morning. Early." Unable to hold his gaze, she addressed Mr. Harrison as she described her late-night episode on the balcony.

"Let me get this straight," Tim interrupted. "You saw a man walking up the slope in the middle of the night, and you didn't think that was odd?"

"At first I thought he might be a local looking for loot dropped from skiers on the lift, you know?" She avoided looking at him, not wanting him to see that she was remembering how they'd done that a couple of times themselves, searching for lost treasures by the light of the moon.

"Locals don't typically turn on the chairlifts."

His cool, professional tone sent heat to Liz's face. "When the lift started running, I figured it was an employee doing an equipment check or something."

"At one-thirty in the morning?"

"Some employees have to work late into the night, especially at the resorts with night skiing." She hated that her voice sounded defensive.

"Eagle Summit doesn't have night skiing," Tim said.

"Well, how was I to know that?" she shot back. "I've been gone three years, you know."

"I know." His mouth clamped shut on the last word.

"Do you think the deceased is an employee?" Mr. Harrison seemed alarmed at the thought. "Surely not. It must be a snowboarder who snuck by the lift operator during the final sweep yesterday, trying to get in one last run. At least—" he paused to swallow hard "—that's what I thought until I heard Miss Carmichael's story."

Tim nodded. "We'll need to pull the daily logs and verify that the operators on duty yesterday recorded a good last chair, but if what Liz says is true, I'm guessing the end-of-day procedures will all check out."

"Maybe it was somebody trying to do a little unauthorized night skiing," Liz suggested. "Some of those extreme boarders are crazy, you know."

Liz snapped her mouth shut. No need to remind Tim about the nature of snowboarders. He had been an extreme snowboarder and skier during college. He'd skied anything and everything that had even a thin layer of snow, inbounds if he had to, out of bounds preferably. He and his buddies had worked as part-time lift operators, not for the pay, but for the free lift passes.

Why couldn't she just keep her mouth shut and resist the urge to remind Tim of the past? For some crazy reason Liz wanted to jab at him, to cut through that professional mask and get a glimpse of the Tim she knew so well.

Tim ignored the jab. From the corner of her eye she saw him watching her, but she refused to look at him. Instead, she focused her attention on Mr. Harrison.

The poor guy looked as if he might faint. He bent at the waist and planted his elbows on the counter to drop his forehead onto his hands. "This is terrible. Think of the publicity."

Odd reaction, considering someone had died. "Publicity?" Liz asked.

The resort owner nodded without raising his head. "I know, I know. What a self-centered response, and completely mercenary. Some poor man froze to death right here on our property. I'm sorry for him and his family, I really am. But do you know what this is going to do to us?" He tilted his head to look up at her without straightening. "We're barely making our payroll as it is. If word of a death at Eagle Summit gets out, who's going to want to ski here? This could sink us."

At the sound of rustling behind her, Liz turned in time to see Grandma stride through the door. The outrage on her face sent Liz backward ten years to the time she and Debbie were fifteen-year-olds caught joyriding around the neighborhood in Grandma's new Buick. Thank goodness Grandma had another target in her sights at the moment. Though Liz felt sorry for Mr. Harrison.

Grandma planted herself inside the doorway and speared the resort owner with a searing gaze. "Young man, I'd like a word with you."

The man straightened and managed to look like an aging delinquent in a suit and tie. "Yes, ma'am?"

"My granddaughter has decided to ignore my advice about moving the wedding to a more *suitable* location." A single flare of her nostrils left no doubt as to her opinion on that matter. "So it appears the wedding party will be staying here after all, as arranged."

Mr. Harrison let out a quiet sigh. "I appreciate that, Mrs. Carmichael."

"I'm sure you do. However, I just attempted to check in and was told by the impertinent girl at the front desk that a room won't be available until four o'clock." She brought her wrist up before her face to glance at her watch in a deliberate gesture. "That is *eight* hours from now. Unacceptable, sir. Quite unacceptable."

Mr. Harrison hurried around the counter. "A misunderstanding, madam. I assure you, your suite is ready, and I think you'll be pleased with it. I've personally selected all the accommodations for the bridal party, the best the lodge has to offer. I'll make sure the staff understands you and your guests are to receive VIP treatment."

"Hmmph." Grandma's sniff indicated her willingness to be mollified, especially if she could enjoy VIP status. She caught Liz in her gaze. "When you're finished here, Elizabeth, join Deborah and me in my *suite*. And don't be too long."

She followed Mr. Harrison out of the shop, leaving Liz and Tim alone. Five awkward seconds was all Liz could handle before she headed for the exit.

"Liz!"

She stopped, but did not turn. Silence stretched between them. Liz fought the urge to look at him, to see his expression. But she'd taken all of the cold glances she could handle from him this morning. She would *not* turn around and face another one.

Finally he spoke. "Don't go far. The sheriff will be here in a minute. He'll want to talk to you." His voice was flat, impersonal.

The same voice he'd used three years ago, the day their engagement crumbled.

Throat tight, Liz gave a single nod and left the coffee shop.

SEVEN

Tim stood inside the front entrance, watching for the sheriff's car. When the white Durango pulled beneath the awning, he stepped outside.

"Richards." Sheriff Zach Daniels stood from the driver's seat and folded muscled arms over his barrel chest. "What's the situation?"

Tim straightened to his full height and still had to raise his chin slightly to look the six-four sheriff in the eye. "Everything's quiet down here. Word hasn't gotten out yet. The body's up at the top of the lift." He briefly outlined the information he'd learned from the teenager, the sheriff nodding as he listened. "The owner, Mr. Harrison, has arranged for a snowmobile to take you up."

Sheriff Daniels's gaze swept over Tim's ski suit. "You off today?"

"Yes, sir. But I'll stick around if you need me."

Daniels gave a curt nod and leaned into the car to grab the radio. He requested a deputy to be dispatched to Eagle Summit Resort before tossing the radio back inside and slamming the door closed. "Hang close for a little while. Somebody will relieve you shortly."

The man strode toward the door without waiting for an answer. Tim fell in step behind him. Inside, a handful of skiers marched across the lobby toward the rear door, their ski boots clattering on the tile floor. Mr. Harrison, hovering beside Liz near the front desk, spotted Tim and the sheriff and hurried in their direction.

"I'm Greg Harrison," he said. "My wife and I own Eagle Summit Resort."

Sheriff Daniels shook the man's hand. "I understand a body has been found on the premises." His voice boomed throughout the lobby. The skiers skidded to a stop and turned to stare.

Harrison winced and spoke in a low voice. "If you don't mind, can we step into my office to talk? I'd prefer not to alarm the guests."

He led them to an office beyond the front desk. When he opened the door and gestured for them to enter, Tim followed the sheriff into a large room with no windows and only two chairs—one behind a cluttered desk and one in front of it. Sheriff Daniels strode without hesitation to the high-backed desk chair. Tim crossed to stand against the opposite wall, turning in time to see Liz precede Harrison through the door. The sheriff noticed her and turned a questioning glance on Tim.

"This is Liz Carmichael," Tim said as Harrison closed the door. "She arrived in Park City late last night and witnessed something that might prove helpful."

The sheriff's stern expression relaxed into a warm smile when he looked at Liz. Tim shifted his weight from one foot to the other. His attractive former fiancé frequently had that effect on men. Daniels rose and extended a hand across the desk.

"Miss Carmichael, I'm Zach Daniels, Summit County Sheriff. It's a pleasure to welcome you to our town."

Liz took his hand. "Thank you, Sheriff."

He gestured toward the chair, and Liz seated herself, placing her purse on the floor beside her. Harrison came to stand against the wall beside Tim, while Daniels slid back into the desk chair.

"Where are you from, Miss Carmichael?"

"Portland originally, but I live in Kentucky now." She perched on the edge of her seat, hands clasped tightly in her lap. "Though, I'm not a stranger to Utah. I went to college at the U."

"Ah, a fellow alumni from the University of Utah." Sheriff Daniels leaned against the chair back. "But I'm sure you were there long after me. I probably graduated about the same time as your grandfather."

Tim saw Liz's rigid posture relax a fraction as she returned his smile. "I doubt that. You're not nearly old enough."

"You'd be surprised." He propped his elbows on the arms of the chair and steepled his fingers. "I've never been to Kentucky, but I hear it's beautiful. Where do you live?"

Tim watched as the sheriff drew Liz out with a few minutes of chatter, admiring his technique that put her completely at ease. He effortlessly extracted the reason for Liz's trip to Utah and the details of her arrival in Park City. Tim would have jumped in with, "Describe what you saw" immediately, but he recognized the wisdom of Daniels's approach. A calm witness was much easier to question. Only when Liz relaxed enough to rest her back against the chair did he bring the conversation around to the point.

"So tell me about last night, Miss Carmichael. Deputy Richards said you saw something that may be important?"

The sheriff's first mistake, though an unwitting one. At the mention of Tim's name, Liz glanced sideways at him and her shoulders stiffened.

She can't stand to be in the same room with me.

Which was completely unfair. After all, who was the injured party here? Who got dumped three weeks after announcing their engagement to his friends and his whole family? Who was left looking like a chump? He gathered his eyebrows into a scowl as Liz gave a halting account of her midnight view from the balcony.

Sheriff Daniels let her finish before uttering a word. "Interesting. Did you notice what he was wearing?"

"A bulky jacket, probably a ski jacket. It might have been black or some other dark color. I…" She squeezed her eyes shut. "I don't know about the rest. I want to say jeans, but I can't be sure. They could just as easily have been ski pants."

"And snowboarding boots?"

She nodded, then hesitated. "I—I think so. I mean, if he was carrying a snowboard, surely he had on the boots."

"About how big was the snowboard he carried? And how did he carry it?"

She shot Tim another quick glance that stabbed at him. Did the sheriff's question bring to mind for her the time she helped him shop for the right size of snowboard, as it did to him? Her lips tightened for a moment before she answered. "I can't say for sure how long it was. Four and a half feet, maybe? He carried it lengthways, under his right arm as he walked."

"And then you saw the lift start to move."

"After a little while."

"How long after?"

Liz's expression grew doubtful. "I don't really know."

"An estimate," Daniels prompted. "It could be important. Five minutes? Ten? Half an hour?"

"Not half an hour." She shook her head. "About twenty minutes, maybe?"

The sheriff pursed his lips and rocked in the desk chair for a few seconds, his unfocused gaze on her. Then his smile returned and his eyes refocused. "Anything else?"

Liz shook her head. "Not that I can think of." She looked down at her hands in her lap. "I'm afraid I wasn't very much help."

"Every piece of information helps us build a clearer picture of the events surrounding the crime. We appreciate your help." Daniels gave a huge rock forward to launch himself out of the chair. Tim stood straighter, and beside him Harrison stepped forward as Liz picked up her purse and rose.

"If you remember anything else, give me a call." He fished a card out of his badge case and handed it to Liz. "I'm sorry you received such an unpleasant welcome on your return to our state, Miss Carmichael. I hope the rest of your trip is pleasant."

"Thank you, Sheriff."

Liz took the card and stepped toward the door. As Harrison reached for the knob to open it for her, a quiet tap sounded. The woman from the front desk stood on the other side.

"Ski patrol is outside with the snowmobiles you asked for," she told Harrison. "To take you up to the, uh, the…"

Harrison rescued her. "Thank you, Kate. We'll be right there."

With a nod of farewell toward the sheriff, Liz left without another glance in Tim's direction. An unreasonable stab of disappointment shot through him as he watched her walk away.

Harrison gestured through the doorway. "If you're ready?"

Daniels rounded the desk, and as Tim fell in beside him, he spoke in a low voice. "Were you rough on that girl before I got here?"

Tim started. "Of course not. She approached me after she heard the news, and told me the same story you just heard."

The sheriff's eyes narrowed. "She seemed nervous around you."

Tim set his teeth together. He kept his eyes forward, aware that Daniels studied him as they walked. "We have a history."

After watching him for a few more steps, Sheriff Daniels gave a single nod. "I wondered."

Discomfort gnawed at Tim as he stepped back and let his boss exit the office first. That man was way too observant.

* * *

Liz quickstepped across the lobby, eager to put some space between her and Mr. Harrison's office—or rather, the people inside Mr. Harrison's office. In all her obsessive worries the past few months, she had known she would have to face Tim during this trip. It was bound to happen, since he was Ryan's best man. But she sure didn't anticipate being thrown so closely together with him so soon after her arrival. Or that he would be so stone-faced every time she looked at him.

What did you expect? Hugs and kisses? You dumped the guy for one of his friends.

An inward cringe kicked up her pace, so she was practically running when she rounded the corner that took her away from the lobby—and away from Tim.

Every time she looked his way, guilt stabbed at her. Guilt—and something else. But she didn't want to think about what that might be. She'd much rather subject herself to a day spent in Grandma's acerbic company.

The elevator doors slid open as her finger reached for the button. Jazzy and Caitlin stood inside, their faces lighting when they caught sight of her.

"There you are," Jazzy said. "We were hoping to see you before we took off for the day. Where have you been?"

"Talking to the sheriff." Liz waved vaguely in the direction of the office she'd just left. "He wanted to hear about that guy I saw last night."

She tried to sidle past them into the elevator, but Caitlin grabbed her arm and pulled her aside. "Oh, no, you don't. You're not getting away that easily."

"Yeah, we're not letting you escape without an explanation. You were engaged to a tall, dark, handsome dreamboat and you never told us?" Jazzy held up a hand and crooked her fingers. "C'mon. Dish."

The elevator doors swooshed closed. Liz spared a longing

glance at them. Eventually she'd have to come clean to her friends about the disastrous ending of her relationship with Tim, but right now she didn't think she could talk about him. Not when he was just around the corner, a few yards away.

"Listen, I promise I'll tell you all about it later. But right now I've got to get up to my grandmother's room before she has a cow." She let her gaze travel from Jazzy's eyes to Caitlin's, silently pleading with them to let her off the hook.

Tenderhearted Caitlin conceded first. "Okay, we'll save our questions for tonight." She placed a warm hand on Liz's arm. "But now we know why you were so reluctant about this trip. Are you going to be okay?"

"I'll be fine." Liz put more confidence in her tone than she felt.

She would be fine. As long as she kept her distance from Tim.

Two snowmobiles waited outside the back door, the drivers in their red ski patrol jackets standing nearby. Tim zipped up his ski suit as he followed Sheriff Daniels toward them. He noticed a few skiers staring at the sheriff on their way to the nearby chairlift, skis perched on their shoulders.

"That the one over there?" Daniels nodded toward the chairs gliding upward.

"No. It's that one." Harrison pointed in the opposite direction, beyond a thick tree line.

The lift he indicated was not moving. Tim glimpsed an empty chair, a double, suspended from thick wires just beyond the tops of the pine trees. From down here he couldn't see more than one chair. He glanced at the balconies lining the building they'd just exited. Assuming Liz's room was on one of the upper floors, she probably had a good view of five or six chairs before the cable disappeared beyond a dip in the slope.

They arrived at the vehicles and Harrison gestured toward the waiting patrollers. "They'll take you up to the top."

"You're not coming?" Daniels's tone voiced disapproval.

"My wife manages the ski resort," Harrison explained. "She's up there now, where they found the—" he gulped "—him. She'll be able to answer your questions better than I."

Daniels nodded and approached the closest machine. "I'm expecting another deputy any minute now. He'll need to get up there, too."

One of the patrollers stepped across the bench seat of his snowmobile. "It's a quick ride up to the top of Crested Eagle. I'll drop you and come back."

Tim mounted the machine behind the other ski patroller and held on to the seat back. They let the snowmobile carrying the sheriff lead the way across the flattened snow. Cold air blew in Tim's face as the machine gained a little speed. If he'd known he'd be going to the top instead of an on-duty deputy, he'd have grabbed his ski mask and gloves out of his truck. It was going to be even colder up there.

A young woman wearing a green ski suit with the Eagle Summit logo emblazoned on her chest stood at the far edge of the building in the center of the trail leading to the Crested Eagle lift. Probably assigned to send skiers back to the other lift. The girl stood aside to let them pass, and Tim nodded as they zipped by her.

· When they rounded the bottom line of trees, the terrain slanted slightly downward toward the Crested Eagle lift's loading ramp. He'd skied here many times, but now he looked at it with eyes sharpened by the discovery of a body. Behind him, a line of pine trees effectively blocked the view of the lift hut from the lodge's parking lot. Liz must have seen the guy crossing the trail for no more than a dozen steps. He glanced behind him at the ruts their snowmobile runners left in the snow. Could they pinpoint the exact place the man crossed by his footprints? Probably not. Some skiers put on their skis and poled from the lodge to the lift, but most walked, carrying their skis and boards. There would be dozens or even hundreds of prints.

Even so, Tim continued to scan the ground as they approached the lift hut. He saw what might have been deep boot prints in the soft snow at the edge of the trees, but he zoomed past before he could be sure. Another Eagle Summit employee, a lift operator, stood guard at the hut. The young man leaned against the side of the building, but leaped to attention as the sheriff zipped past. The door to the hut stood open, and Tim glanced at the machinery inside.

The Crested Eagle lift wasn't long, only a hundred chairs or so. The runs it serviced were mostly advanced—steep, deep and usually bumpy, exactly the kind he liked. Green skiers stayed away from this part of the mountain, preferring the gentler slopes on the other side.

The run beneath the lift was no more than a hundred yards wide. Tim kept his eyes on the trees to his right as they climbed to the top. They were thick and full. He'd skied in there often enough to know that there was a narrow trail down the center, with just enough room for sharp turns as you glided downward. The snow in there was always soft and deep—a joy to a competent skier.

A small crowd stood near the hut at the top, huddled close together well away from the unloading ramp. Tim glanced at them long enough to note five people before his gaze was drawn to the figure lying on the snow-covered ramp. The body lay on its side facing away from him, the legs bent in a sitting angle.

The snowmobile carrying the sheriff came to a stop by the group, and Tim's drew up beside it. The roar of the engines died away as Tim climbed off the bench seat. The silence of his immediate surroundings was broken by the distant echo of voices, skiers enjoying a day on the slopes, unaware that a man lay dead close by.

A woman stepped forward, her straight, chin-length dark hair sprinkled liberally with gray. Her snow boots left no imprint on the packed snow as she approached the sheriff.

"I'm Emma Harrison."

Daniels took her gloved hand. "We met your husband down at the lodge. He said you manage this ski resort?"

"That's right." Her gaze flicked toward the body briefly, before returning to the sheriff. "We've never had anything like this happen, though. I'm not sure what we're supposed to do next."

Daniels gave her a comforting smile. "We'll figure it out together. First let's take a look at what we've got here."

From the look on her face, Mrs. Harrison wasn't eager to get any closer to the body than necessary. She stayed where she was when the sheriff stepped around the snowmobile. Tim followed, his boots crunching on the snow.

When they drew near, the sheriff squatted down beside the body and examined it closely. Tim stayed back a couple of feet to give him room. A dark ski cap covered the man's head and had slipped down over his eyes.

"What's this?" Daniels reached out and carefully lifted the ski hat to peer beneath it. He drew a sharp breath. When he twisted around, his eyes pierced Tim's.

"Richards, call dispatch. Get a team out here now." His voice held an unmistakable note of command. His gaze shifted to Mrs. Harrison. "I want this resort shut down immediately. Get every skier off the mountain."

Tim looked down at the body, his hand frozen in the process of unzipping the pocket that held his phone. A piece of critical information, hidden by the ski cap, had not been relayed to the kid who broke the news about the body.

This was no nighttime snowboarder who'd accidentally frozen.

The man had been shot through the head.

EIGHT

Standing in the carpeted hallway in front of the door to Grandma's suite, Liz took a moment to gather her courage. She resolved to be pleasant, no matter how trying her grandmother became. This was a special time for Debbie, and Liz wasn't going to be the cause of family strife. Besides, now that Grandma had gotten her chastising out of the way, maybe they could put the issue of the brooch behind them and enjoy the day.

She straightened her shoulders and rapped her knuckles against the door. It swung open immediately.

Debbie heaved an exaggerated sigh in her face. "Finally! Where have you been?" She shifted her eyes toward the room behind her and mouthed, "She's driving me crazy."

Liz stepped forward and folded her cousin in an embrace. "Sorry," she whispered, then went on in a louder voice. "The sheriff wanted to ask me a couple of questions. But that's over, and I'm ready to go. What's on the agenda today?"

"The sheriff?" Grandma's sharp voice snapped across the room. "What did he want with you?"

Liz released Debbie and stepped into the room. The layout of Grandma's suite was exactly the same as hers, though the furnishings looked newer. From the e-mails Debbie had been sending for months about the plans for this week, Liz knew that her mom and dad would stay in the second bedroom with Grandma when they arrived on Friday. She also knew Mom wasn't thrilled about the arrangement, but since Grandma had volunteered to foot the bill for the out-of-state family's hotel and airfare, she was prepared to make the best of it.

Liz stepped into the living area and dropped onto the sofa beside her grandmother, her purse still slung over her shoulder. "I saw a snowboarder out on the slopes last night. The sheriff just wanted to hear about it in case it turns out to be the same person they found this morning."

Grandma's sharp eyes narrowed. "You're not planning to involve yourself in another scandal, are you, Elizabeth?"

Another scandal? Liz bristled, but at the sight of Debbie's anxious expression, bit back a quick reply. She forced a pleasant smile to her face. "Of course not."

"Good." Grandma gave a firm nod. "Deborah doesn't need anything else to mar her wedding. A death on the premises is quite enough. And I still think we should find another location."

Debbie's jaw tightened. Despite her irritation, Liz bit back a smile. Apparently, she and her cousin were going to spend the day calming each other down from Grandma's verbal barbs.

"So." Liz slapped her hands on her jeans and stood. "Where to first?"

"The florist," Debbie answered. "I want to check on the bouquets and boutonnieres, and I need to make the final payment."

"It's ridiculous what they charge for wedding flowers." Grandma scooted to the edge of the cushion and held her hand out for Liz to help her stand. "And why you insisted on fresh I'll never know. They'll be gone in a few days, and what will you have left?"

"Pictures," Debbie answered instantly. "And lovely memories."

"You'd better get some good pictures, for what that photographer is charging you." Liz helped Grandma heave herself up off the sofa. "It's a racket, I tell you. The florists and the caterers and the photographers all got together and formed a conspiracy to fleece brides for every penny they have. Outrageous." She headed for the bedroom. "Let me get my coat and hat and I'll be ready to leave."

When Grandma disappeared into the other room, Debbie grimaced. "She's right, you know. Take my advice, Liz. When it comes your turn, go on a cruise and get married on the beach in Jamaica. It's got to be cheaper."

Liz refused to acknowledge the image that rose in her mind at the mention of her wedding. She'd had such plans…once.

"I'll keep that in mind," she told her cousin.

Duke sat in his car, his gaze fixed on the front entrance of the lodge. The sheriff's Durango made an ominous specter parked directly beneath the awning. It was risky being here while the police were running around the place, but according to his partner, there wouldn't be a better opportunity than this morning. And besides, the sheriff would be up on the top of the mountain looking at the body, not running around in the hallways of the lodge.

If Sinclair hadn't been such an amateur, Duke wouldn't have to dirty his hands with this. But he'd learned a lesson in his dealings with the two-bit thug: Rely on no one. The men he was playing with now wouldn't tolerate unprofessional behavior.

Where was that girl? He glanced at his watch. Anxiety tightened his hands into fists. He couldn't wait around much longer.

The doors swung open. Three figures stepped outside.

She was one of them.

Instinctively, Duke slid lower in the seat. The old lady was a stranger, but he'd met the other girl. As long as she didn't spot him he'd be okay. His breath came in excited gulps. This was going to work out.

The trio headed toward him. For a short, breathtaking moment it looked like they might walk right up to his car, then they turned and crossed to a row of handicapped parking spaces. The family resemblance between the two girls was pronounced. Same height, same build, same dark hair. He examined the musician.

You're in my territory now, Kentucky girl.

His hand strayed to the bulge in his ski jacket where the gun nestled in the inside pocket next to his heart. The girls followed the old woman to a maroon Taurus with Utah plates and climbed in. He waited until the Taurus backed out and pulled away.

When they had disappeared from sight, Duke turned the ignition key and started his car. The way he figured, he had at least half an hour. Plenty of time, as long as his partner had given him the right room numbers.

"There's one right there, Elizabeth." Grandma's finger stabbed at the windshield. "I assume you know how to parallel park?"

Liz eyed the space Grandma indicated. It looked pretty small. She would have preferred to park in the garage the next street over, but Grandma didn't want to walk up the steep incline of Park City's Main Street to get to Alpine Jewelry. And she had flatly refused to let Liz drop her off in front of the shop. After listening to Grandma berate the florist over the scandalous price of white roses for the past half hour, Liz didn't want to give her any further cause to argue. She caught Debbie's eye in the rearview mirror and received a supportive wink. After a quick silent prayer, she maneuvered the Taurus back and forth into the parking space.

She shoved the gearshift lever into Park and turned a victorious smile toward Grandma. "There."

Grandma opened her door and looked out. "You're a little close to the curb, but at least you didn't hit anything." From Grandma, that almost counted as praise.

Main Street in the historic mining town boasted an eclectic collection of shops, some touristy, most outrageously expensive, all trendy. Liz had spent a lot of time here with Tim when they were dating, investigating every store on the steep street and wandering through the small art galleries. As she rounded the front of the car to follow Grandma and Debbie into the jewelry store, it was all she could do to keep her gaze from straying uphill toward their favorite pizza restaurant. There, seated at the little table by the window, was where Tim first told her…

No. I'm not going there.

A tone announced their presence when Debbie pushed the door open. Liz followed Grandma inside and let the door swing shut behind her. The heat in the shop stung her cheeks, a startling but welcome contrast to the frigid temperature outside. Glass display cases lined both walls of the narrow shop, their sparkling surfaces gleaming in the fluorescent lights. A collection of clocks decorated the walls, some new, but most appeared to be well-cared-for antiques. Liz even saw an old-fashioned cuckoo clock.

A clerk seated over a worktable behind the rear counter looked up. "May I help you with something?"

"I'm here to pick up a ring," Debbie said. "The name's Carmichael."

A man came through an open doorway next to the worktable. "I'll take care of it, Christy." He shifted his gaze to Debbie and smiled. "How are you, Miss Carmichael?"

"I'm fine, thanks."

"Getting nervous about the big day?"

Debbie dimpled. "Not yet, but I still have a few days for the jitters to set in." She glanced at Liz and Grandma. "Mr. Cole is the manager, and a very talented jewelry designer. He designed my engagement ring and did a beautiful job." She straightened her arm in front of her to admire the ring. "Mr. Cole, this is my grandmother and my cousin from Kentucky."

"A pleasure to meet you both." He shook Grandma's hand first, and then took Liz's. He held it in an icy-cold grip for a moment, a polite question in his blue eyes. "All the way from Kentucky? I hope you're going to have a chance to enjoy something of Utah before you head back."

"I'm just here for the wedding," Liz replied, "but I think we're going to ski at least one day."

"We sure are," Debbie said. "Tomorrow all the bridesmaids are hitting the slopes at Eagle Summit together. It'll be fun."

"I'm sure it will." He stepped toward the back room. "Will you be picking up both rings today?"

Debbie shook her head. "Just Ryan's. He'll be in to get mine soon."

"I'll be right back."

He left, and Grandma said, "Girls, come look at this."

Liz stepped up beside her and looked down into the display case. Dozens of pieces of jewelry lay artfully arranged on velvet. The gleam of jewels winked up at them, sparkling with an array of colors from beds of gold, silver and platinum. Liz let out a breathless "Ah!" as she admired the beautiful rings, bracelets, pins and pendants.

"Look at the design of that bracelet." Grandma's voice held a note of awe as she tapped on the glass with a heavily ringed finger. Grandma had a weakness for jewelry, as evidenced by the amount she wore and the overflowing jewelry cases Liz had loved looking through as a young girl. "Notice the braided gold, the way the emeralds are woven into the pattern. It's absolutely stunning."

Liz agreed. She had never seen anything quite so lovely. "And look. There are earrings to match."

"I told you Mr. Cole was talented," Debbie said.

Grandma looked up, her eyes gleaming nearly as much as the gemstones beneath the glass. "He designed these pieces?"

Debbie nodded. "He showed them to us last year when he was working on my ring. He fixes expensive watches and antique clocks, too." She pointed toward the collection on the walls.

Mr. Cole returned at that moment. "Here you are, Miss Carmichael. Please inspect the inscription and make sure it's exactly what you wanted."

He handed a small box to Debbie, and while she looked inside the ring, Grandma tapped on the display case. "Mr. Cole, am I to understand you are the man who created the pieces in this case?"

He looked modestly down at the jewelry display. "Do you like them?"

"They're nice enough," Grandma answered in an off-handed tone. "Tell me, what do you get for a piece like…oh, let's say, that bracelet there?"

Liz turned away to hide her grin. If there was anything Grandma loved more than jewelry, it was haggling for a bargain. If she could combine the two she'd be as happy as a cat in a fish market the rest of the day. Which meant maybe she'd be easier to get along with.

While Mr. Cole took a key ring from his pocket and unlocked the door in the rear to show Grandma the bracelet, Debbie grabbed Liz's arm and pulled her away.

"Look at this." Debbie handed her the wedding ring, her eyes suddenly as full of sparkles as the jewelry on display. "Can you believe in just a few days I'll be Mrs. Ryan Baxter?"

Liz took the ring carefully. A row of small diamond chips

studded one side of the simple gold band. Inside, the inscription read "God blessed me with you."

"It's great, Debbie." She handed it back with a smile and folded her cousin in a hug. "I'm so happy for you."

She really was genuinely happy. If only she could put her own tumultuous emotions about this trip aside and focus on Debbie. But the longer she was in Utah, the more those emotions tried to surface. And the harder Liz had to fight to keep them at bay.

If she could just manage to stay out of Tim's way, she'd be okay.

NINE

Tim's ears had gone numb with cold. He pulled his hands out of his pockets and tried to warm them with his palms. At least his ski suit was warmer than the other deputies' uniforms. He cast a sympathetic glance toward the tree line, where two men with equipment bags painstakingly searched the snow for signs of a trail leading from the trees to the chairlift.

He stood beside the sheriff at the bottom of the Crested Eagle lift and watched an evidence tech snap pictures of the machinery inside the hut. The man's fingerprint kit lay on the snow, ready for use. Tim doubted they'd need it. The person who entered the building would surely have worn gloves— ski gloves, probably. But it was an exercise that had to be performed to satisfy the rules of the investigation.

"Look at those scratches." The sheriff held the padlock toward Tim. "Think someone might have picked the lock?"

Tim wasn't wearing gloves, as the sheriff was, so he examined the object without touching it. It was a heavy-duty lock, a two-and-a-half-inch body with a steel shackle. Nothing at all remarkable about it. You could buy them in any hardware store. The sheriff held the keyhole toward him, and Tim noted the scratches on the casing.

"Could be," he agreed. "But those could also be made through normal usage by a key scraping across the metal."

The sheriff cocked his head sideways, looking closer. "Maybe so. The owner says all the keys are accounted for."

Tim glanced at the lift operator hovering nearby and spoke in a lower voice. "Which might mean it was opened by someone with a valid reason for having a key." Mrs. Harrison had also told them that the padlocks in use all over Eagle Summit Mountain were keyed alike. That might indicate that the killer was an employee, or at least someone with access to an employee's keys.

Assuming it had been the killer who put the dead man on the lift and sent him up the mountain. Tim wasn't comfortable making any assumptions at this stage of the game. They had too many unanswered questions, and very few facts.

For instance, since the dead man wore ski clothing, they assumed he'd come to the mountain for some unauthorized night skiing. But where were his skis and poles? They hadn't found them near the body. Tim had personally ridden with a ski patroller slowly down the run beneath the lift, and hadn't seen a sign of any equipment that may have been dropped from a chair. Nor had he seen any sign of blood spray on the snow or on the chair that had carried the body to the top of the mountain. Which might indicate the man had been dead when he was put on the lift. But if so, where was he shot? And why would the killer drag the body to the lift? It made no sense.

"Sheriff Daniels, we found something." Excitement pitched Adam Goins's voice high, making it carry clearly across the snow from the area near the trees where he searched.

Daniels glanced at Tim and set off across the slope at a slightly uphill angle. Tim followed.

"Careful," shouted Farmer, the deputy working with Goins. "Come straight toward us." He aimed his hand in a straight path across the snow between them. "If you veer left you're going to walk across the prints."

Tim searched the snow as he walked. Strong winds last night had blown off a lot of the fresh snow that fell yesterday afternoon. Nearest the lift, the surface was hardpack powder, scarred by the signs of an uncountable number of skis. Impossible to see an individual trail. But the closer they drew to the trees the softer the snow became, and he found what could possibly be identified as boot prints. Faint and nearly obscured, but getting deeper the farther they walked. None of the telltale gouges a skier wearing ski boots made as he dug hard heels into the snow. These prints looked like…

Snowboarding boots.

"Sheriff, look at that." Tim pointed toward the ground.

The sheriff nodded, but did not stop. He spoke without turning his head. "I saw."

As they neared the pair by the trees, Goins gestured toward the ground. "Someone came out of the trees here. Look. It's a perfect set of prints."

He was right. Tim noted a couple of deeper boot prints in the softer snow that bordered the actual ski run, just inside the tree line. They'd been obscured, but not obliterated by a smoothed-down swath about twelve inches wide that ran right over the top of them. The pattern looked familiar.

"That was made by a snowboard." He looked at the sheriff. "This had to be the same person Liz saw last night. Whoever made those prints was pulling a snowboard behind him to cover his prints. And the boots were snowboarding boots. The regular kind, not the kind with a step-in binding. Like these."

Tim lifted one foot and showed the bottom of his boot to Sheriff Daniels and the other deputies.

Daniels pursed his lips as his gaze slid from Tim's boot to the prints. "A snowboard sliding across the snow wouldn't be heavy enough to smooth down the snow like that."

Goins spoke excitedly. "It would if it had the weight of a body on it. Take a look at that."

Tim looked where he pointed. A little way beyond the smooth swath, the clear lines from the snowboard disappeared beneath a double line of uneven gouges. Tim approached cautiously from uphill and stooped to examine the snow more closely. He could still see the edges of the indentation made by a board.

"It looks like something was dragging behind the board." He looked up and caught Daniels's gaze. "Like legs, maybe? Our dead guy was wearing ski boots, and those would leave a trail like this."

The sheriff sucked in his cheeks and stared at the snow. His eyes moved as he traced the trail into the trees.

Tim followed his gaze. Was that where their mysterious skier met his fate?

"Richards, you're dressed for a hike in the snow." Daniels dipped his head toward Tim's ski suit.

Tim spared a glance at Goins's and Farmer's uniforms and boots. Solid work boots, great for riding around in a cruiser and for walking on packed powder. But they'd sink up to their knees in the soft snow between the trees, and those cotton uniform trousers weren't very thick.

"Yes, sir."

Tim stepped off the firm ski run toward the trees. The ungroomed snow gave under his weight. He moved gingerly, feeling the snow scrunch beneath his thick rubber soles, staying several feet away from the track left by what he was convinced was a snowboard carrying a body. Between the trees, the swath of smoothed snow was clearer, easier to identify.

"We need to get a camera in here," he called back toward the sheriff. "The trail is well defined."

"I'm on it," Daniels answered.

Tim continued. This line of trees dividing two ski runs was wide, at least a couple hundred feet across, and the pine trees grew thick. Within a few feet he came across a narrow ski trail, the snow packed by skiers gliding through the trees on their way to the bottom of Crested Eagle, or maybe down to the lodge. The prints he followed disappeared over the trail, but picked up again in the loose snow on the other side. Tim ducked under a low-hanging branch and kept going.

Through the center of the dense patch of forest ran another ski trail, this one even narrower than the first. Tim had used it to cross from one ski run to the other when he'd skied this resort, though most skiers preferred the safety of the wide-open slopes. Only experts risked the danger of skiing in the trees. An out-of-control skier could smack into a trunk and be severely injured or even killed. It had happened more than once. Tim liked tree skiing because of the softer snow, and the privacy the deep foliage provided. The pine boughs also created a natural sound barrier. Skiing in the trees, you could almost imagine you had the mountain to yourself.

Something unnatural caught his eye up ahead. Anticipation prickled the skin beneath the collar of his ski suit. Was that a pole? He hurried forward, careful to keep a safe distance between him and the item that had snagged his attention. As he drew near, he saw that it was, indeed, a ski pole standing upright, the tip planted in the snow. On the ground beside it rested its mate. And leaning neatly against the nearest tree, as though placed there in anticipation of their owners' return, stood a pair of Salomon X-Wings.

The track he'd been following ended just beyond the skis, in a wide spot in the trail. A quick glance around the small clearing settled a sick feeling in his stomach and confirmed his suspicion. This is where their dead guy had met his end.

He turned his head to shout over his shoulder in the direction of the sheriff. "I found it."

Daniels's voice came to him from the distance, muffled by the trees. "Found what?"

Acid churned in Tim's stomach as he stared at the unmistakable evidence before him. Blood-soaked snow and a blood-splattered tree trunk left no doubt.

"I found the murder scene."

TEN

"That was delicious." Liz slid her jacket zipper all the way up to her neck when a cold breeze slapped her in the face. They'd just left the restaurant Debbie had hired to cater the reception.

"Quite acceptable." Grandma hooked a hand through Liz's arm as they prepared to cross Main Street. "Though I'm sure the prices are far too high."

Liz glanced toward Debbie, who simply lifted a shoulder. She'd insisted on ordering for them, then grabbed the check and refused to show Grandma. Liz knew she didn't want to put up with the complaints that would surely have followed.

Liz changed the subject to head off any pointed questions.

"I still can't believe you talked Mr. Cole down to almost half price on that bracelet." Liz gave her grandmother an admiring glance as they walked up the steep sidewalk.

"You robbed him." Debbie, walking on the other side of Grandma, managed to look disapproving and impressed at the same time.

Grandma tilted her chin upward. "Nonsense. He made a nice profit on the deal. I'm sure his markup on those pieces is ridiculous. How much did they cost to produce? Just the price of the gold and the gemstones."

"And hours and hours of labor." Debbie's eyes clouded as

she shook her head. "I hope he wasn't offended. He's really an artist. It must be terrible to bargain down on something you've spent hours creating."

"Nonsense," Grandma repeated. "He's pleased to find an admiring audience for his work. Think of the publicity he'll receive when I wear my bracelet and tell everyone where I got it." She patted the handbag hanging from the crook of her arm with a gloved hand.

Debbie looked like she wasn't ready to let the argument drop. She opened her mouth, but Liz gave her a stern glance over the top of Grandma's leopard-print fleece hat. Their elderly relative actually wore a satisfied smile. Why risk a return of the harangue?

Debbie must have sensed her reasoning. She shut her mouth.

Liz glanced into the store windows they passed. Many new shops had opened since she was here last. Her favorite art gallery had been replaced by a Western wear clothing store that boasted a display of suede, boots and rhinestone-studded blouses in the front window.

She spoke without thinking. "Things sure have changed since Tim and I hung out here."

Grandma snorted. "They certainly have. A *lot* of things. I must say, I was surprised you could hold your head up this morning after the shameless way you ended your engagement to that poor boy."

Liz's cheeks stung as though she'd been slapped. This was exactly why she'd dreaded this trip. Bad enough she had to face Tim. Why must her own grandmother constantly throw her sins in her face, as well?

"Grandma!" Debbie's tone was sharper than Liz had ever heard it. "Would you leave Liz alone? I'm sure coming back to Utah was hard enough as it is. She doesn't need us making it harder."

Loyal Debbie. Liz sniffed, thankful for the cold breeze that might explain the tears prickling in her eyes. "What do you think I should have done, Grandma? Like Debbie said this morning, marriage is a huge commitment."

"Of course it is. We Carmichaels have never had a divorce in our family." Her eyes narrowed as she looked sideways at Liz. "And we never will."

"I know that." Liz nodded. "And I didn't want to be the first. Too many marriages fail these days, even Christian marriages. I see it all the time. I figured it was better to back out of the engagement than risk breaking a lifetime vow to Tim... and to God."

There. Maybe Grandma would let the subject drop with that explanation. No need to dredge up the reasons Liz had been concerned that her marriage to Tim wouldn't last.

But Grandma was never one to let a barb go unflung.

The elderly lady stomped forward a few paces, her jaw set. "Well, you certainly could have chosen a better way to end it, that's all I have to say. Your behavior was shameful."

Debbie sucked in a noisy breath. "Grandma, would you stop throwing Liz's past in her face? Let it go."

Mouth pursed, Grandma gave a single nod and fell silent. Liz tried to give her cousin a grateful look, but Debbie wouldn't meet her gaze. She stared straight ahead, her lips tight. Guilt turned the good lunch into concrete in Liz's stomach. Debbie might defend her loyally, but Liz knew her cousin had never understood why she broke off her engagement to Tim. And she definitely didn't approve of the way it had come about.

Of course, Liz didn't blame her for that. What kind of heartless person dumped a guy for his friend?

ELEVEN

"Right through there, boys. Those snowmobiles will take you up to the site."

Tim stepped out of the way as the county medical examiners followed the sheriff's directions through the lodge toward the rear exit. He'd just finished filling out the required paperwork, detailing the events of the morning. Sheriff Daniels held it in his hand, and kept rolling it absently into a tube.

The Harrisons stood nearby, anxiety apparent in their worried expressions and tightly clasped hands. When the MEs had filed past, each carrying a bulky equipment bag, the resort owners hurried toward the sheriff.

"How long will it be before we can reopen the slopes?" Mrs. Harrison's voice quivered as she looked up at the big man.

Sheriff Daniels's expression remained impassive. "We'll work as fast as we can. If all goes well, you should be back in business by Friday."

She clutched at her husband's arm. "But that's two days away."

A stab of sympathy shot through Tim. "That's the worst-case scenario, ma'am. They might finish up today, and then you'll be able to reopen tomorrow."

Tim glanced at the sheriff for confirmation. He gave a single nod.

Mr. Harrison's throat moved as he swallowed. "Let's hope so."

A voice intruded on their conversation from the direction of the front desk. "Our package included lodging and five days' worth of lift tickets. That's what it said in the ad. Now, what are you going to do about it?"

Tim turned to see a man and woman in ski gear glaring across the counter at the desk clerk.

Mrs. Harrison moaned, and Mr. Harrison patted her arm. "I'll take care of it." He hurried away to rescue the harried-looking clerk and soothe his angry customers.

Her eyes followed her husband. "We're buying them all lift tickets to one of the other resorts, and offering a free shuttle to anyone staying here." Deep lines creased her brow as she looked at Tim. "But we can't afford to do that for more than one day."

The Harrisons' preoccupation with finances had struck Tim as a bit mercenary at first, but looking into her worried face now, he realized their financial situation must be dire. They weren't unsympathetic, just concerned for their business, their livelihood.

If only there was some comfort he could offer. He wanted to tell her he would pray for her and her husband, but with the sheriff's hulking presence, he didn't think that would be appropriate. Instead, he plastered on a confident smile. "I'm sure they're working as fast as they can. Don't lose hope."

She gave a distracted nod. "I'd better get back to the ticket office. My team is probably pulling their hair out, dealing with all those angry skiers." She hurried in the direction of the back door.

The sheriff shook his head as he watched her go. "I sure feel sorry for those folks. Hope we can wrap this up today."

Tim's nod followed the MEs. "Think they'll be able to tell us anything quickly?"

"Nah. It got down close to zero last night. Probably colder in a chair forty feet off the ground. Body's frozen solid. Makes pinpointing the time of death nearly impossible. We're going to have to wait for the autopsy to find out anything for sure."

"Well, let's hope we can get an ID from his prints through BCI."

The Bureau of Criminal Investigation was the best chance for identifying the victim quickly. A careful search of the body had revealed no identification of any kind. The lift ticket attached to his ski jacket was an afternoon, half-day pass purchased yesterday at the Eagle Summit ticket window. The resort used the old-fashioned method of punching a hole in the ticket as a skier loaded the first lift of the day, so there were no electronic scanning systems to see when the man arrived.

Sheriff Daniels's eyes narrowed as he looked sideways at Tim. "What are you still doing here, Richards? Supposed to be your day off, isn't it?"

"I thought I'd stick around for a while, you know?" Tim lifted a shoulder. "See if I can be useful."

The sheriff clapped him on the back. "You've been useful enough. I appreciate your help, son. But I've got your report, and if we need any more information from you, I know how to get ahold of you. Now get out of here. Go ski, or board or whatever you were planning to do today."

Ryan had sent Tim several text messages asking when he was going to meet up with the guys. He felt guilty for ditching his best friend, but this was the department's first murder investigation since Tim became a deputy. A far cry from the car burglaries and security alarm calls he normally took. Gruesome though it might sound, he kind of hated to miss out on it. But the sheriff obviously didn't need him hanging around.

He nodded. "I guess I'll take off, then. Thanks, Sheriff."

"Good timing, son." Daniels nodded toward the lodge entrance.

Tim turned, and through the doors he saw a white van with an unmistakable antenna on top come to a stop beside the sheriff's Durango, still parked beneath the awning. The side door slid open and a man carrying a large camera on his shoulder jumped out.

"The circus is about to begin." The sheriff straightened his collar, his eyes on the reporter headed his way.

Some aspects of police work held no appeal for Tim, and television interviews topped the list. It suited him just fine to leave that job to Sheriff Daniels.

He lifted a hand in farewell. "I'm outta here. Call if you need me."

As he left, he held the door open for the cameraman and an eager-looking woman holding a microphone. Having caught sight of Sheriff Daniels inside, they hurried by him without a second glance.

Tim escaped to his truck, glad for the anonymity of his ski suit.

Liz followed Debbie down the hallway to her condo, cradling the bottom half of the wedding dress. The garment was safely zipped in a special bag to protect it from stains, but the wedding gown consultant had cautioned them that the delicate organza and satin would be easily crushed or creased, and they shouldn't let it drag. In her other hand, Liz carried the crinoline, which she held high above her head. Her arms ached with the strain. Who'd notice a crease in the crinoline, anyway? But after a whole day with Grandma, her normally even-tempered cousin was starting to show signs of strain, so Liz had decided to do as she was told and keep her opinions to herself.

"I had no idea wedding dresses were this heavy," she commented as Debbie stopped before her door.

"I know. Imagine what I'm going to feel like by Saturday night, walking around with that thing on."

"You look beautiful in it, though."

Debbie flashed an eager smile as she fished the key out of her purse. "Do you really think so? It doesn't make me look fat?"

Liz laughed. "Like you could ever look fat. You're going to be the most beautiful bride ever, and I've seen a lot of them."

Gratitude deepened Debbie's smile. "Thanks, Liz. I just wish you were one of my bridesmaids."

"No way. We agreed years ago, when we were kids, that I'd play my cello at your wedding and you'd sing at mine." She hefted the crinoline higher, trying to find a new position for her aching shoulder muscles. "Besides, I look awful in pink, you know that."

"You do not." Debbie fitted the key into the lock, twisted and pushed the door open. "Besides, if you'd been one of the bridesmaids, I would have chosen blue, to match your eyes." She stopped. "By the way, I am *not* going to ruin my dress with that hideous pin. So you just make sure you hold on to it until after the ceremony, okay? Then I'll put it on for one picture to keep Grandma happy."

Debbie had never liked the heirloom brooch. But then again, Debbie wasn't into jewelry, as Liz had always been.

Liz grinned. "You've got a deal."

They stepped inside the condo and Liz followed her cousin into the bedroom. The dress and the crinoline filled half of the empty closet. Debbie fussed with the bags, making sure they hung straight, while Liz dropped onto one of the double beds.

"Will the rest of the girls be here tonight?"

"Uh-huh." Debbie ran a hand down the bag one last time, then turned. "They had to work today, so they'll miss dinner, but they're going to meet us over at The Java Hut later."

Liz threw herself backward across the bed and covered her eyes with an arm. "I halfway wish I could miss dinner tonight, too. When did Grandma get to be so cranky?"

"What are you talking about?" The mattress heaved as Debbie dropped onto the bed beside her. "She's always been cranky."

"No, she's worse than she used to be." Liz moved her arm to look at her cousin.

Debbie's expression grew cautious. "Honestly? It's that stupid pin. She's been obsessing about it for weeks."

Liz let out a disgusted grunt and sat up. "I tried to give it back to her when Tim and I broke up. She wouldn't take it." She plucked at a loose thread on the comforter. "It's not my fault she gave it to me too early."

Her tone came out whinier than she intended. When Debbie covered her hand and squeezed, she looked up into a sympathetic smile.

"Have you ever wondered if you made a mistake? Especially when…" She bit her lower lip and looked away. "You know."

Liz did know. "You mean especially when I got dumped just a month later?" She let out a harsh blast of laughter. "I got what I deserved, didn't I? I'm sure everybody said so."

She didn't mean the words to sound so bitter, but a flood of unpleasant emotions she'd worked hard to ignore for three years was threatening to slip past her carefully erected barrier. She launched herself off the bed. Now was not the time to deal with those feelings.

"Liz, I never said that."

Something in Liz's chest loosened, and a prickle at the back of her eyes warned of oncoming tears. She could handle accusations and Grandma's caustic comments, but the compassion in Debbie's voice was something she couldn't handle right now.

She whirled to head toward the doorway. "Listen, I've got to check in with my friends. We're supposed to go over our music before dinner. So I'll see you at six-thirty in the lobby, right?"

Silence from Debbie's direction. Liz turned at the threshold to look at her cousin. Debbie stared across the room, head tilted at an angle as she regarded her open suitcase on the other bed.

"Six-thirty, okay?" Liz repeated.

"Yeah, okay." Debbie raised a finger and placed it over her mouth, still staring at the suitcase, clearly confused about something.

Liz looked at it. "What's wrong?"

"N…nothing." Uncertainty gave the word three syllables. "It's just that I thought I zipped my makeup case in the inside pocket."

Liz stepped over to the suitcase. She picked up a rainbow-colored pouch resting atop a neat stack of clothing in the suitcase's main compartment. She held it toward her cousin. "This?"

"Yeah. I grabbed a lipstick out of it this morning before we left." The lines cleared from Debbie's forehead. "Oh, well. I must not have put it back where I got it." She gave a silent laugh. "Maybe the wedding jitters are getting to me after all."

Liz tossed the bag back into the suitcase. "Probably."

Debbie followed her across the condo's main room. She opened the front door, and when Liz stepped into the corridor, she spoke. "Hey."

Liz turned. Debbie leaned against the doorjamb, watching her with a sympathetic expression. "I know it must be weird for you, seeing Tim after all this time. I was half-afraid you wouldn't come, and I've been praying for you like crazy. I just want you to know how much I appreciate it."

Liz wrapped her in a hug. "Don't talk crazy. I wouldn't miss your wedding for anything." Once again, she held the tears back by sheer force. This trip was proving to be even more emotional than she'd anticipated. "I love you, girl."

When the embrace ended, Liz smiled goodbye and headed down the hall toward the condo she shared with her friends. She pulled the key from her shoulder bag, but when she fit it into the lock the door whipped open.

Jazzy stood inside. Liz started to laugh at her white raccoon mask above a terribly sunburned nose, but then she noticed her friend's expression. Jazzy looked like she'd seen a ghost.

Alarm tickled in Liz's belly. Had there been an accident on the slopes? "What's wrong? Is Caitlin okay?"

"She's fine." Jazzy gulped, the fear in her round eyes swallowing the rest of her face. "But someone has been in our condo."

TWELVE

An icy drop of fear slid down Liz's spine. It was happening again.

"Would you stop saying that, Jazzy?" From across the room, Caitlin chided the petite violinist with a stern look. "You don't know that."

Jazzy's dainty chin rose. "I do, too. I know the exact position I left my pajamas on my pillow. They've been moved at least an inch sideways."

From anyone else, that statement would have made Liz laugh. But Jazzy was a neat freak, the most fastidious person Liz had ever met. Her obsession with order bordered on compulsion. If Jazzy said someone had moved her pajamas, Liz believed it.

She closed the door behind her and glanced around the condo, fearful of what she would find. But everything seemed to be in order. The couch cushions, the table lamps, the appliances on the kitchen counter, everything looked exactly as it had when she left this morning.

"Is anything missing?" she asked. Alarm shot through her. "Is my cello okay?"

She raced into the bedroom. Her cello case lay on the spare bed where she had left it this morning. Or had it been moved? Was it closer to the pillows than it had been?

The clasps on the case were firmly closed. Liz dropped her purse on the mattress and snapped them open. She let out a relieved sigh at the sight of the polished maple instrument. She lifted it gently out of its velvet lining and turned it over. Everything seemed to be fine. Both her bows were still secured in their holders, and a quick check of the accessory pocket assured her that everything—rosin, mute and endpin rest—was still there.

When she'd replaced the cello in its case, she turned in a circle, examining the room. The top dresser drawer was slightly open. Had she left it that way this morning?

Stop it! Don't overreact.

Caitlin and Jazzy hovered in the doorway and watched as she opened each drawer to check the contents. The task didn't take long, since she'd only brought enough clothing for a few days. Every article appeared to be in order.

"I think everything's here," she told her friends as she slid the last drawer shut. "If someone was in here, they didn't steal anything."

Caitlin folded her arms across her chest. "You two are being paranoid." Jazzy's expression became stubborn, and Caitlin held up a hand to forestall her protest. "I know you have some excuse to be suspicious after the break-in at Liz's apartment and the incident in Waynesboro last year. But in this case, I think you're overreacting. There is no real evidence that anyone has been in this condo except us. Nothing has been taken."

"Nothing was taken from my apartment, either," Liz reminded her.

Caitlin conceded the point with a tilt of her head. "But they trashed your place." Her hand swept the neat room. "Obviously, that hasn't happened here."

Jazzy still looked stubborn. "Maybe they've gotten smarter."

Laughter played around Caitlin's lips. "You think the person who broke into Liz's apartment in Kentucky followed us out here? He'd have to be after something pretty valuable." Her eyes twinkled as she shifted her gaze to Liz. "Have you got the Hope Diamond hidden in your suitcase?"

The Hope Diamond. A tumbler clicked into place in Liz's mind. "Nothing like that," she said slowly, "but I do have my grandmother's brooch."

Jazzy's eyes grew round. "Is it still here? It isn't missing, is it?"

Liz shook her head as she crossed the room and snatched her purse off the bed. "I didn't have a chance to bring it back upstairs before I left with Grandma and Debbie this morning. I've had it with me all day."

She unzipped her purse and pulled out the silky box. Jazzy and Caitlin drew close as she opened the lid. Multicolored jewels gleamed in their golden setting.

"How much is it worth?" Jazzy asked.

Liz lifted a shoulder. "I have no idea. When Grandma gave it to me she called it a priceless heirloom." She tilted the box so the gems sparkled in the light. "I assumed she meant *priceless* as in *irreplaceable,* because it's been in our family for so long. She has a picture of my three-times-great grandmother wearing it on her wedding dress back in the late 1800s, along with a shot of every generation who owned it since."

Until me. Liz let the thought go unsaid.

"So it's over a hundred years old, right?" Caitlin shook her head. "I'm surprised you have the nerve to wear it. I've seen it on you several times."

"Only when we play at weddings." Liz allowed herself a brief and bitter smile. She was supposed to have worn it at her own wedding. "That seemed appropriate somehow."

Jazzy peered at the brooch. "You ought to take it to that *Antiques Roadshow* thing."

"I never wanted to know how much it was worth."

She still didn't, because she knew it wasn't hers to keep. She'd been lucky enough to enjoy temporary possession of the heirloom, but she always knew she'd have to hand it over when Debbie and Ryan married. Because Liz was certain she had blown her only chance at marriage when she broke up with Tim.

She snapped the lid shut and closed her fingers around the box. "I'm positive the value is purely sentimental. My family isn't poor, but we've never been wealthy."

"You can't be sure of the value unless you have it appraised." Jazzy's eyes narrowed. "What if whoever broke in your apartment back in December knew you'd bring it to your cousin's wedding and followed us out here to steal it?"

Liz nodded slowly, giving in to the fearful suspicion that had lurked in the back of her mind since Caitlin mentioned the Hope Diamond. "It's the only thing I have that anyone could possibly want. And there's something you don't know." She let her gaze slide from Jazzy to Caitlin. "I just came from Debbie's room, and she thought her makeup case had been moved while we were gone."

Jazzy let out a noisy gasp. "We need to report this to somebody."

"This is ridiculous." Caitlin's no-nonsense tone broke the tension in the room. "For one thing, that person would have to know about the family tradition of passing along the brooch. And not only that, they'd have to know Mrs. Carmichael had given it to Liz three years ago, and that Liz would bring it with her to Utah." She turned a stern look Liz's way. "We're your best friends and we didn't even know about it. You two are letting your imaginations get the best of you." She put a hand on her hip and faced Jazzy. "And just what would you tell the police? That someone came into our condo while we were gone and moved your pajamas an inch to the right?"

Her friend's levelheaded logic worked on Liz's nerves, and she felt herself beginning to relax. Caitlin was right. She and Jazzy were probably imagining things.

Even so, it wouldn't hurt to find out the value of the brooch, would it? If it was worth more than they thought, Debbie would need to know so she could keep it secure. And it just so happened Liz had met a jeweler today. Maybe she'd run over to Mr. Cole's place tomorrow after she went skiing with Debbie and her friends, and see what he could tell her.

In the meantime, no sense taking chances. She'd do as she'd done today and keep the thing with her. She dropped the box back into her purse and zipped it closed.

Judging from Jazzy's stubborn expression, she wasn't quite ready to let the subject drop.

"You know what we haven't done?" Caitlin looped an arm through Liz's elbow and the other through Jazzy's. "We haven't prayed. The Bible tells us not to be anxious. Let's go sit on that comfortable couch and turn this over to the Lord." She pulled them gently toward the living room.

Liz allowed herself to be swept along. *Leave it to Caitlin to put everything in perspective. Jazzy's always been an alarmist. I should remember that.*

"Well, okay." Reluctance sounded in Jazzy's voice. Then she turned a shrewd glance on Liz. "And when we finish, Liz can fill us in on all the details about her mysterious past with Tim Richards."

A groan escaped Liz's throat. She should have known her friends wouldn't let her off the hook.

"That was delicious," Uncle Jonathan declared as they exited the restaurant that night.

Liz agreed. Grandma selected a local steak restaurant with a quiet atmosphere, perfect for a family get-together. Liz hadn't seen Uncle Jonathan in years, and enjoyed getting to know Ryan's parents, as well. Caitlin and Jazzy, graciously included in the dinner invitation by Grandma, answered everyone's polite inquiries, but Liz saw them both hiding yawns as the meal progressed. Their day on the slopes was taking its toll.

"We're going to call it a night," Mr. Baxter told the group huddled on the sidewalk outside the restaurant.

"I'm glad we finally got to meet you, Liz. We've heard so much about you." Ryan's mother included Jazzy and Caitlin in her smile as she wrapped a wool scarf tightly around her neck against the chill. "I can't wait to hear you girls play."

"Nice to meet you, too, Mrs. Baxter." Liz nodded at her as she took her husband's arm. "See you Friday night at the rehearsal."

"I'm going home, too," Uncle Jonathan announced as the couple walked away.

"Are you sure, Daddy?" Debbie stepped closer to Ryan, shivering in the cold winter breeze. "A bunch of us are heading over to the Java Hut. The girls are probably there now."

"I don't think so. Some of us have to work in the morning. But I'll see you tomorrow night, sweetie." Uncle Jonathan planted a kiss on Debbie's cheek, shook Ryan's hand and then folded Liz in a hug. "It's good to see you again. We've missed you."

Liz smiled into the face that looked so much like her father's. "I've missed you, too."

He looked at Grandma. "Mother, are you going to stay up late and party with the young people?"

"Goodness, no." Grandma held on to her leopard-print fleece hat with one gloved hand as she shook her head. "If I drink coffee this late I'll be awake for three days. You can drop me off at the lodge on your way out of town."

"We'll take you, Mrs. Carmichael." Caitlin shot an apologetic glance toward Debbie, and then shifted it to Liz. "I'm worn out, and I think Jazzy's asleep on her feet."

"I am not." But Jazzy's eyelids drooped, and she wavered as Liz looked her way. "Okay, maybe I am a little tired. And stiff." She arched her back. "Skiing is harder than I thought."

"Take my advice," Ryan told her. "Make sure you have some ibuprofen to take in the morning. You're going to hurt in places you didn't even know you had muscles."

Jazzy groaned. "I think I already do."

The four who were done for the night turned left after the Baxters and headed downhill toward their cars. Liz fell in step beside Debbie and Ryan. Multicolored lights strung in a zigzag pattern across the street twinkled overhead as they marched upward toward the espresso bar at the top of Main Street. Small trees in planters, their leaves stripped by winter, glowed with rows of tiny white lights on every bare branch, like an army of naked Christmas trees. The cold air smelled strongly of burning wood from fireplaces all over town. Tourists filled the sidewalk, laughing and talking as they walked from shop to shop.

Ryan opened the door for the Java Hut and held it as Debbie and Liz stepped inside. The place was crowded, as Liz had known it would be. On weekends, this was a favorite hangout among college students after spending a day on the slopes. Liz had been here often during her years at the U. But tonight the crowd was comprised mostly of vacationers wearing furry winter boots, turtlenecks and expensive ski jackets. Their noisy chatter warred with the hiss of the espresso machine behind a wide counter.

A waving hand drew Liz's attention across the room. "There's Betsy," she told Debbie, pointing out their university friend, who was one of Debbie's bridesmaids.

"Oh, good. They got a table in the back." Debbie waved an acknowledgment. "And look. Patrick's here, too." The redheaded groomsman sat across from Betsy.

Liz and Ryan followed her as she weaved her way through the coffee sippers. Since leaving Utah, Liz had kept in touch with few of her friends from college, most of whom she'd met through her cousin. The three who huddled around the table had been among Debbie's closest friends since high school. They all rose to greet her with hugs.

"Girl, it's been too long," Betsy told her as they sank back into their chairs. "I want to hear what it's like living out there with the hillbillies. Do they really walk around barefoot and carry shotguns all the time?"

Liz laughed. "I can't vouch for the mountain people in eastern Kentucky, but where I live nobody carries a shotgun. And we don't have outhouses, either. Lexington is a city pretty much like Salt Lake, only smaller."

Patrick gave her a wry smile. "Funny how people get a mind-set about a place. You'd be surprised how often out-of-state people ask me how many wives I have when they find out I'm from Utah."

They all laughed, and Ryan left to order three cappuccinos at the counter. Across the table from Liz, Betsy's grin circled the room. "Isn't this fun? Just like old times." She caught sight of something behind Liz's head, and her eyes widened. "Uh, look who's here."

Probably Tim. Liz drew a steadying breath before turning in her chair. She'd already steeled herself for an evening in the chilly company of her ex-fiancé.

But the man who approached was not Tim.

Her stomach dropped to her shoes.

She whirled back around to assault Debbie with a fiery glare.

Debbie's eyes had gone round as giant cappuccino mugs. "Honest, Liz. I had nothing to do with this."

Searching her face for any signs of duplicity, Liz conceded that her sweet cousin wouldn't play such a dirty trick on her, nor would Ryan. And judging by the awkward expressions the girls wore, they didn't have anything to do with it, either. Which meant Jeremy Norville, the man who had lured her into breaking off her engagement and then dumped her a month later, had showed up on his own.

Probably to torment her.

"There's the beautiful bride." Jeremy's voice boomed across the noise in the restaurant as he made his way to the table. "I saw your man fighting the crowd at the counter."

"Hi, Jeremy." Debbie accepted his kiss on her upturned cheek, watching Liz. "Uh, what a surprise. I figured you'd be down in the valley, working long hours on a research project or something."

"I ought to be." Jeremy had landed a job as a statistical researcher for the State of Utah shortly after they graduated. "But you know what they say about all work and no play." Jeremy's gaze slapped at Liz across the table. "Besides, I couldn't pass up the chance to see Liz, could I?" He turned the full weight of his beseeching grin Liz's way.

"You didn't mind missing opportunities to see me in the past." The words snapped out before she could stop them.

A hurt expression overtook his features. "Aw, c'mon, Lizzie. Surely you're not still nursing a three-year-old grudge."

She'd hated that pet name since grade school, when the kids teased her about it. She could still hear their taunts: "Lizzie Borden took an axe…" Jeremy was the only guy who had ever used it, the only one she'd let get away with it since sixth grade. But he had lost the privilege a long time ago.

"Please don't call me that." She spoke carefully, through gritted teeth, aware that everyone else at the table was looking awkwardly down at their coffee mugs, or staring at the table's scratched wooden surface.

"Sure, Liz, whatever you say." He grabbed the chair next to hers and turned it around backward to straddle it facing her.

"Don't be angry with me. We were friends. Can't we let by-gones be bygones?"

He was so close she could smell his minty breath. To her surprise, his proximity wasn't as terrible as she'd thought it would be. Jeremy had always taken full advantage of those Irish green eyes and dark hair, and Liz could feel his charm starting to thaw the edges of her outrage.

She couldn't hold a grudge against Jeremy for breaking up with her. She'd known, down deep, that he wasn't after a lifetime relationship. He had never promised that. No, she realized a long time ago that the fault belonged squarely with her. She was the one who had dumped Tim for his friend. She had broken up not only her engagement, but also a longtime friendship. It was only right that Jeremy dumped her in return. A perfect example of street justice in action.

In the depths of the laughing eyes that were fixed on her Liz glimpsed something. Sincerity, maybe? Perhaps Jeremy really was sorry for what happened. Maybe coming here tonight was his way of extending an olive branch. That couldn't be easy for him, just as it wasn't easy for her to be around Tim.

Realizing that this was as close to an apology as she was likely to get from him, Liz forced a smile. "Okay. Bygones it is."

She extended a hand to seal the deal. But he gave her one of the cockeyed grins she remembered so well, the one that used to melt her insides.

"Oh, I think we can do better than that."

He leaned over the back of the chair and planted a lingering kiss on her cheek. It was a pleasant surprise to realize that the touch of his warm lips on her skin didn't stir her at all. She fixed a relieved smile on him.

"Ahem."

They both turned, as everyone around the table looked up.

Ryan stood beside them holding a tray with four steaming mugs, his eyes round. At his side stood Tim.

Her gaze drawn to his, a sickening shock coursed through Liz. That he'd seen Jeremy's kiss was obvious. Tim's face was pale as his eyes flicked between the two of them. He wore the expression that still haunted Liz's nightmares, the one that flooded her with gut-wrenching guilt. The same stricken expression he'd worn the day he found her and Jeremy locked in a passionate embrace.

Liz was unable to hold his gaze. She turned away.

Jeremy, at least, seemed determined to keep the awkward situation light. "Hey, there. I was up here on an errand and thought I'd stop by for a shot of espresso to keep me awake on the drive home. I saw the gang back here, and just came over to say hi." He jumped out of the chair. "Here, buddy, let me give you a hand with that."

Wordlessly, Ryan yielded the tray and Jeremy set it on the table in front of Liz. The back of her neck burned from Tim's gaze. No way was she going to turn around and face him with Jeremy in the same room. She grabbed for one of the mugs and gulped the scalding liquid. It scorched her throat on the way down, a pain she welcomed as a just reward for the agony she'd just seen in Tim's eyes. Across the table, Debbie sat with her mouth gaping open.

"Don't run off on my account," Jeremy said. "I'm not staying."

Tim was leaving? Liz couldn't stop herself. She twisted in her seat.

But all she saw was the back of Tim's coat as he left the espresso bar.

The door of the Java Hut whooshed closed behind Tim. He didn't pause even a moment, inhaling the frigid night air as he walked away from the restaurant. Fast. He needed to put space between him and that worm who used to be his friend.

The rational part of his mind whispered that the kiss he'd just seen was harmless. Platonic. Nothing like the one he'd interrupted three years ago.

But the irrational part sent emotions coursing through his brain that he was powerless to control. Anger. Hurt. And above all, white-hot jealousy.

What were the chances of walking into the Java Hut at that exact moment?

Lord, haven't I suffered enough at that guy's hands?

He broke into a run, willing the cold winter air to cool down the searing heat that roiled in his soul.

THIRTEEN

When Liz and her friends exited the elevator the next morning, the sound of voices in the lobby was almost as loud as in the espresso bar last night. People crowded the front desk, and Kate, the woman on the other side of the counter, looked frazzled. Piles of luggage and ski bags littered the tiled floor.

"What's going on?" Jazzy asked. She was moving gingerly this morning, but she'd taken Ryan's advice about the ibuprofen and insisted she was up for another day of skiing.

"I don't know." Liz hooked her finger in her ski jacket and slung it over her shoulder. She carried her backpack in her other hand. "Looks like they're all checking out."

"Poor Mr. Harrison." Worry lines creased Caitlin's smooth forehead. "I feel so sorry for him."

Liz pointed across the lobby. "Let's head for the coffee shop. We're supposed to meet Debbie and the other girls in there."

They threaded their way through the people and luggage. When they stepped through the door of the coffee shop, the sound of chatter from the lobby diminished. A television set hung suspended from the ceiling, the volume turned up loud enough to echo in the empty restaurant. Mr. Harrison stood behind the counter beside an older woman, both of them staring up at the screen where a female reporter looked directly into the camera as she spoke.

"…dead on a chairlift at Eagle Summit Mountain Resort in Park City. The victim has been identified as thirty-seven-year-old Jason Ronald Sinclair of Utah. Sinclair reportedly died from a gunshot wound to the head."

The scene changed, and Brandon, the kid Liz had seen yesterday in this very coffee shop, directed a toothy grin at the camera. A snow-covered slope showed in the background. Behind the counter, Mr. Harrison emitted a strangled moan.

"The dude was dead, and like, Popsicle City, you know?" the teen told the reporter. "My buddy was at the top of the lift, and I was at the bottom, and we got the all-clear to start it up, and then this body came up on chair thirty-seven. My buddy thought it was, like, a joke, you know? But it sure wasn't no joke." Brandon's voice took on a tone of ghoulish glee. "It was a frozen dead guy."

The reporter's voice sounded again as the camera angle switched to sweep over the tree-lined slope with an unmoving chairlift in the background. "Eagle Summit Mountain Resort closed down yesterday on orders from the Summit County Sheriff, but is expected to reopen this morning. We've been told the sheriff will make a statement at ten o'clock, and we'll be here with live coverage. I'm Sara Reese, Channel Two News."

The broadcast returned to the newsroom and the smiling faces of a male and female anchor behind a neat desk. Liz turned toward Mr. Harrison, who had collapsed onto his folded arms over the coffee shop counter, while the older woman patted his back.

"We're done." The man's voice was muffled by his sleeves. "We might as well close our doors."

Liz gave Caitlin and Jazzy a worried look. *The poor man.* She put a hand on his arm. "Surely this will blow over. Business might be lean for a day or so, but then people will forget."

He shook his lowered head. "I don't know if we can

weather the storm for even a few days." He peeked upward and spoke in a lowered voice. "My wife thinks it's a conspiracy. Someone's trying to put us out of business."

Killing some poor man and planting his body on a chairlift seemed like a pretty elaborate way to shut down a business to Liz. Unless the man they found was somehow associated with the resort.

"Did you know the victim?" she asked. "This Jason Sinclair guy?"

"Never heard of him."

Caitlin gave the top of his head a sympathetic smile. "Then a conspiracy theory seems a little far-fetched."

Jazzy agreed. "Besides, you never know. You might get more business than normal out of this." Mr. Harrison lifted his head to give her a questioning look. "You know, people love to do something spooky. Some might come just so they could ride on the chair the body was found on."

Mr. Harrison was still staring at her with something like horror when Debbie and the rest of the wedding party arrived, their heavy ski boots clattering on the tile flooring with every step.

"There you are." Debbie leaned her skis and poles against the rear wall. "What a zoo out there."

Betsy and the other girls lined their skis up beside hers.

"Oh!" Mr. Harrison stood and straightened the knot of his tie beneath his chin. "I deserted poor Kate to watch the news. I need to get out there and help her."

He hurried away, passing Ryan and his friends on their way in as he exited.

"Wow, what a mob." Ryan set his snowboard on a table. "If all those folks are leaving, this place is going to be a ghost town by tonight."

Patrick rubbed his hands. "Good. We'll have the slopes to ourselves. No lift lines."

The woman behind the counter frowned in his direction and disappeared into the back room. Liz echoed her frown. She was all for short lift lines, but didn't the guy realize how self-centered he sounded? Besides the fact that Mr. and Mrs. Harrison could be ruined financially, someone had been killed. Murdered. And the killer was still out there. Celebrating short lift lines was shallow at best, in addition to being naively ignorant. She was about to say something along those lines when someone else entered the coffee shop and her words dissolved.

Tim was here.

She'd tossed and turned through most of the night, unable to clear her mind of the wounded expression on his face when he'd seen her and Jeremy together at the Java Hut. Her emotions had run the gamut from guilt (this was the second time she'd injured the man, and he didn't deserve it) to indignation (after all, they had no ties, no commitments, so why shouldn't she greet an old friend?) to anger (was he going to hold her past mistakes over her head for the rest of her life?). Somewhere around three o'clock she'd come to a horrifying realization. Jeremy was no threat at all. She'd been able to look at him without feeling even a twinge of the attraction that had been such an irresistible force three years ago. He was safe.

But Tim was not safe. Definitely not. She couldn't even look him in the face. She didn't *want* to be attracted to him, but when he walked into a room she felt his presence like a physical assault. Her head went light. Her heart throbbed in her ears. Her blood roared through her veins at light speed.

Like now.

"Hey, there's my best man." Ryan extended a fist in greeting.

Tim knocked his knuckles against Ryan's. Liz kept her eyes turned away, but she strained to watch him through her peripheral vision. He balanced his snowboard on the floor on one end and nodded a greeting around the room. After a quick glance, he did not look in her direction.

"What's going on out there?" He jerked his head toward the lobby.

"The proverbial rats." Patrick shook his head. "They've decided this ship is sinking, and they're bailing out."

"Hey, Tim." Ryan leaned against the pastry case. "The morning news said the sheriff found out who the dead guy was. You know anything about him?"

"Nope." One of Tim's eyebrows rose. "But if I did, I couldn't say anything. You know that."

Though Tim wasn't looking at her, Liz felt the weight of Debbie's stare. The bridesmaids also kept throwing her curious glances. She ignored them all. The only females who weren't aware of last night's disastrous episode were Jazzy and Caitlin. They were both asleep when she came in, and she didn't want to talk about it this morning.

"So." Liz's voice came out too loud. "Where are we skiing today?"

"I'm sticking to the blues and greens," Debbie announced. "The last thing I need is to break a bone on a black diamond two days before my wedding."

"That's fine with me," Betsy said, and the others nodded their agreement.

"What are blues and greens?" Jazzy asked. "I didn't have the nerve to ask my instructor yesterday. It's like everybody here speaks a foreign language."

Debbie smiled at her. "It's just a classification system for skiers. The easy slopes are marked as greens. Blues are a little harder, so only skiers who've advanced to the intermediate level take those. And blacks are the really hard ones."

Jazzy's mouth twisted. "So I want the green ones?"

"Actually," Liz answered, "there's a bunny slope with a slow chairlift for beginners."

With a quick look toward Jazzy, Caitlin gave Liz a know-ing smile. "We'll probably hang around the bunny slope this morning and see how it goes. Can we meet up for lunch somewhere?"

"Sounds like a plan," Ryan said. "There's only one slope-side restaurant, Nellie Belle's Café, at the midmountain lodge. Want to meet around eleven-thirty?"

Liz knew Caitlin had skied before, and had been looking forward to this trip. "You know, I haven't been on the slopes in three years. I think I might need to hang with the bunnies this morning, too. Caitlin, you go on up with Debbie and the girls. Jazzy and I will see you at lunch."

Debbie opened her mouth to protest. Having hung out with Tim and Ryan for four years during college, Liz had become an expert skier and Debbie knew it. Liz gave her a loaded look and shifted her eyes for a moment toward Tim. Debbie shut her mouth without speaking. Though Liz didn't relish the thought of hanging out on the beginner slopes, at the moment it seemed far better to spend the morning with Jazzy than trying to avoid loading a lift chair beside Tim.

Liz tried to ignore the look of relief that flooded Tim's face. And the answering disappointment that deflated her. He didn't want to spend time in her company, either.

The morning was even tougher that Liz expected. Poor Jazzy tried, but she was a pretty dismal skier. By lunchtime, Liz's arms ached from pulling her friend up off the snow from one face-plant after another. As they rode the Old Baldy Express up to midmountain, Liz decided she'd stayed on the beginner slopes long enough. It was Caitlin's turn to babysit the bunny skier for the afternoon.

"I'm never going to get it," Jazzy moaned.

"Sure you will. You're doing great for your second day on

skis. It took me a week to get my turns, and you just about had it on that last run."

"Really?"

"Really," Liz lied.

Jazzy looked down. This lift was the first one she'd ridden outside of the bunny slopes, and her expression showed her anxiety as she stared at the ground forty feet below them.

"We're pretty high up in the air, aren't we?"

"Oh, not that high." Liz kept her tone worry-free.

"And we're moving really fast."

The beginner lift was so slow it had driven Liz crazy all morning. "That's why they call it a high-speed lift. It's going to take us up to midmountain."

"What if I don't get off in time?" She twisted in her seat to watch an empty chair returning on the downhill line. "Can I just stay on it and go around again?"

Liz bit back a laugh. "They really don't like you to ride down, just up. But don't worry. It'll slow down at the unloading ramp. Do it just like you've been doing it this morning. Stand up and lean forward. You'll be fine."

"If you say so." Jazzy sounded unconvinced.

Truth be told, so was Liz. They'd had a couple of near catastrophes getting off the slow lift already today.

As they approached the lift hut at the top of the slope, Jazzy scooted to the edge of the chair, her poles clutched in her hands so hard they trembled. Liz tried to be inconspicuous as she scooted as far away from her friend as the chair allowed. Beginners were known to cause some pretty extraordinary disasters getting off lift chairs.

They reached the snow-covered ramp beside a lift hut that looked very much like the one at the bottom of the hill. A sign told them to UNLOAD HERE. Holding her poles in one hand, Liz checked to be sure her backpack wasn't snagged on the chair back. She placed her skis firmly on the snow and leaned forward.

Unfortunately, Jazzy panicked. Her legs went wide, and one ski slid across Liz's. Their legs became tangled, and in a matter of seconds, Jazzy tumbled. In a frantic, last-ditch effort to keep her balance she grabbed for Liz, and down they both went.

From the corner of her eye, Liz saw the lift operator slap the shut-off button. The chair they just unloaded came to a stop dangerously close to their position. A chair whipping around the corner could cause a concussion if it connected to the back of a downed skier's head. Liz tried to disengage her legs, skis and poles, but Jazzy's thrashing made it impossible to get free. They floundered on the snow, and Liz took a blow to the lip. The bitter taste of copper pennies filled her mouth.

She let out an involuntary, "Ouch!"

"Oh, I'm so sorry," Jazzy said. "Here, let me just get my leg out."

"No! Just stop moving!"

The kid running the lift ran over and grabbed Jazzy beneath the arms, dragging her away. In the next moment, Liz felt a strong hand on her arm and an all-too-familiar voice in her ear.

"Here, I've got you. Can you stand up?"

Tim. Her stomach sank. Why did he have to show up in time to see her wallow on the snow like a walrus? Could she manage to look any less graceful?

"Of course I can stand up," she snapped.

Okay, that came out way sharper than she intended. Tim released her arm and stepped away. She righted her skis, planted her poles and hefted herself upright as he watched.

"Whoa, that was spectacular!"

Liz turned in the direction of Ryan's voice and groaned. Everyone was there, standing in a line, watching the show.

"Are you two okay?" Worry saturated Caitlin's tone.

"I'm fine." Liz flashed a quick, miserable smile in Tim's direction. "Thanks."

He nodded, turned, and walked away. Quickly. Like he couldn't wait to get away from her.

"I'm so sorry." The lift operator had hauled Jazzy to her feet, and she duckwalked on her skis toward Liz. "I'll never get this skiing thing."

"It's okay." Liz tried to smile. "Really. Everybody has trouble with the lift at first."

Jazzy looked into her face, and then winced. "You're bleeding."

Liz swiped at the corner of her mouth with a gloved finger. "It's not bad. Don't worry about it." She could already feel her lip starting to swell. Good thing she played the cello and not the flute, like Caitlin.

Ryan glided over to them. "If you two are finished fooling around, can we go eat? I'm starved."

He chuckled. Liz rolled her eyes at him, but managed to hold her tongue.

As the rest of the group began skiing toward the lodge, Jazzy eyed the distance. She gave Liz an apologetic glance. "You go ahead. I think I'll walk."

Liz nodded and pushed off as her friend started taking off her skis.

Yeah, after lunch it's definitely Caitlin's turn to ski with Jazzy.

"Girls, I'm about done in," Debbie announced.

Liz stood at the top of a green ski run with the rest of the bridesmaids. Their skis lined up evenly on the flat snow as they paused to trace the path down the slope they were getting ready to take. A few fellow skiers zipped around them, heading for the bottom.

After a rough morning, the afternoon had been awesome.

No crowds, but more skiers on the slopes than Liz had expected after the mob in the lodge this morning. Caitlin decided to call it a day after lunch, and had accompanied Jazzy to the base of the mountain to get cleaned up and go shopping. The snow was perfect, packed powder, just the way Liz liked it. Her skills, rusty from three years of not using them, had returned within a couple of runs. And best yet, the guys had taken off for the expert runs on the back side of the mountain, so she hadn't had to worry about Tim's glowering presence.

"Sounds good to me. I could use a soak in the lodge's hot tub." Betsy adjusted her ski goggles and gripped her poles. "See you guys at the bottom."

She poled forward and zipped away. The others followed, leaving Debbie and Liz standing at the top.

"I'm going to let the guys know what we're doing." Debbie pulled out her cell phone.

As she keyed in a text message, Liz squinted down the run. If she remembered correctly, there was a trail off to the right that cut over to a black diamond slope she used to like, steep and usually well groomed. Her legs felt great, limber and loose. She'd enjoy doing an expert run.

"I think I'm going to head over to that black diamond." She pointed with the tip of her ski pole to the place where the slope curved. She could just see the beginning of the trail on this side of the location where Betsy was making a turn that took her out of view.

A skier skidded to a stop on the other side of the wide run from Debbie and Liz. He wore a ski mask and reflective goggles. Not an inch of skin showed. His head turned as he traced his own path down. Liz dipped her head in a silent greeting, one skier to another.

"Have at it," Debbie told her. "I'm going to take this nice, easy green all the way down. See you at the lodge?"

Liz nodded and watched as Debbie skied away. She

admired her cousin's moves, her graceful turns, the way her skis carved the snow with seemingly no effort at all.

Alone but for the skier on the other side of the slope, Liz let her gaze sweep the horizon. The Wasatch mountain range surrounded her on all sides. The snow on the peaks in the distance glowed in the afternoon sun. She filled her lungs. The crisp, clean air held a trace of pine. The atmosphere here at eight thousand feet made her alert, supersensitive to her surroundings. She'd always felt closer to heaven in the mountains. A verse from *Psalms* popped into her mind.

Glorious and majestic are His deeds, and His righteousness endures forever.

Glorious and majestic. The perfect description for this piece of God's creation.

Liz pulled her goggles off her forehead and adjusted them over her eyes. She planted her poles and propelled herself forward, her skis sliding easily over the snow. The wind stung her already cold cheeks as she picked up speed on her downhill course. Within a few seconds she approached the entrance to the trail she remembered. She slowed a little and leaned into her turn, pleased with the way her skis responded to the slightest shift of her weight. Then she was on the narrow trail, the trees so close on either side she could have extended her poles and touched them.

Funny how well she remembered this mountain from her college days. It was almost like she'd never left. Gaining confidence, she increased her speed again. The trees zipped by her in a blur.

At the end of the trail, she burst out onto the black diamond slope with confidence. As she executed a sharp left turn to head down the steep run, she glimpsed movement behind her. The lone skier from the top of the last run had come this way, too. Nobody else was in sight.

The snow was not as smooth here. Apparently, the groomers hadn't been over here in a while. At least it wasn't bumpy. But it was a little steeper than she remembered. Liz slowed and focused on making tight turns, controlling her speed with her skis.

Something moved behind her. She jerked her head in that direction. That guy was awfully close. Maybe he wanted to pass.

She crossed to the other side of the slope.

He crossed with her.

Flames of alarm licked at her mind. There was nobody else in sight. Nobody to hear if she called for help.

She leaned forward and tucked like a racer. Her skis flew over the snow. She glanced backward.

He was gaining.

Alarm gave way to panic. Somebody had died on this mountain two days ago.

And this guy was a better skier than she was.

Lord, I need help!

Then the guy was right behind her. Something jerked her jacket. The motion shoved her off-balance. At this speed, she couldn't correct in time. Her skis crossed.

In the moment before she went down, Liz screamed.

FOURTEEN

Ryan cleared the screen on his cell phone and slipped it into his pocket as they neared the lift's unloading ramp. He turned to Tim. "The girls have called it a day. We're supposed to meet them at the hot tub in fifteen minutes."

Tim nodded without committing, using the heel of his boot to knock the ice off his snowboard. Little clumps fell thirty or so feet to the ground as he tried to come up with some excuse or other to head on home. No way was he going to sit in a hot tub with Liz.

After they unloaded at the top, he and Ryan slid to one side, out of the way of unloading skiers, to wait for the other guys. Tim slipped his free foot into the binding on his board and tightened the straps as Ryan relayed the plan to the others. When they were all ready, he hopped toward the downhill slope behind his buddies.

They slid down one green run to the next without pausing. This was pretty tame stuff compared to the experts-only slopes they'd tackled all afternoon. It felt good to cruise down a gentle, tree-lined incline barely steeper than his parents' driveway down in the Salt Lake valley.

As they rounded a corner, they came upon another green run that would take them down to the lodge. The others didn't pause, but managed to grab some air as they soared over the top of the run. Ryan had been hotdogging all afternoon, and had said something about enjoying his last chance to practice stunts before he was forced into responsible behavior. Tim grinned. If Ryan's last fling took the form of nothing worse than a few boarding shenanigans, Debbie had nothing to worry about.

As Tim followed the others, his gaze scanned his downhill path. A familiar figure slipped between the trees just this side of a curve. He'd know that bright pink ski jacket anywhere. He had bought it for Liz himself as a Christmas gift during their last year at the U. She was heading for the steep black diamond south of here that they'd skied together countless times. Liz always did like the steep runs.

Another skier slipped into the trail behind her, but Ryan and the others curved to the left and continued on toward the lodge.

Which he ought to do. Liz obviously wanted nothing to do with him. Even when he was trying to be helpful, she snapped at him.

But she hadn't been on skis in three years. She shouldn't be attempting a black by herself. Despite everything, he couldn't stop himself from worrying about her. If she crashed, she might need help. And maybe if there was nobody else around, she'd be a little nicer about accepting assistance from him.

As Tim approached the trail, he leaped into the air, tucked his knees and executed a sharp right turn into the trees. The narrow, tree-lined trail wound through the forest in wide, easy bends. Liz was too far ahead to see. He caught a glimpse of the other skier as the guy rounded a curve fifty yards in front of him.

Tim flexed his knees to bounce over a series of bumps in the snow. Sanity returned in a flash. What was he doing? Liz certainly would *not* appreciate his help. More likely, she'd be ticked off if he saw her crash, just like before lunch. She'd always been too proud to let him help her, even at the best of times. It was one thing he admired about her, her determination to succeed on her own.

If there was a way to turn around, he should do that now. But this trail sloped downhill, as they all did. No going backward. And the trees were so thick here there was no way to slip between them, either. No, he'd just have to hang back and give her time to get ahead of him and hope she wouldn't see him following her. He slowed.

When he rounded the last wide bend, the end of the trail loomed ahead. Neither Liz nor the other guy was in sight, thank goodness. Just the smooth, steep swath of snow at the end of this narrow path. He'd just take his time getting down this one. Give her time to get ahead of him.

A scream pierced the silence of the mountain.

Liz!

Heart pounding, Tim crouched on his board. He shifted his weight to his forward foot, picking up speed. The wind thundered in his ears.

He burst out onto the slope. His gaze searched the downhill path. There! Liz, unmistakable in her pink ski jacket, lay facedown on the ground. And a man loomed over her. Grabbing at her. Tugging at her clothes.

Tim let out a howl of rage. He didn't have time to think about words, just bellowed like a bear. An *angry* bear.

The guy's head jerked up. Sunlight reflected off his goggles. Tim barreled down the slope, intent on murder. If he harmed a hair on Liz's head…

The guy let go. With lightning speed, he darted away. No doubt an expert on skis. He skyrocketed downhill, and before Tim could blink, he had darted between the trees and was lost to sight.

Indecision warred within Tim. Should he give chase? Or take care of Liz?

No question there. Tim's board shot across the snow in a direct path to his ex-fiancée.

One of her skis had popped off and skittered to the other side of the slope. Her hat and goggles had fallen off or been pulled off, and lay several feet away. She lay facedown on the snow, dark hair sprawled all around her. Her body heaved as she drew in gulps of air.

Tim's heart squeezed in his chest.

He unstrapped his bindings and kicked the board off his boots. Then he threw himself to his knees on the snow beside her and gathered her up in his arms.

"There, baby." The whispered words dropped from his mouth of their own accord. "It's okay now. He's gone. I won't let anything happen to you."

She threw arms around his neck, her sobs loud in his ear.

In that instant, Tim knew. In fact, he'd *always* known.

He was still in love with her.

Rational thought left. One arm holding her close, he ducked his head, tilted her chin with his gloved hand and covered her mouth with his.

For an instant, giddy flutters erupted behind Liz's ribs as her lips softened beneath Tim's kiss.

Then the realization of what was happening broke over her like a thunderhead. She tore herself away with a backward jerk.

Her breath came in ragged heaves as she brought a hand up to her lips, her gaze locked on to his. "What are you doing?"

For one moment, Liz saw something in his eyes. Something uncomfortable. Painful. Something she recognized. A Chinese gong sounded in her ears.

Tim still had feelings for her.

Before she could react to that revelation, his gaze clouded. He looked away. "I'm sorry. I don't know what came over me."

A wave of emotion washed through Liz. Was it fear? Anger? Or maybe…regret?

Lord, what is going on here?

Heart pounding, Liz shook her head. Her thoughts whirled. She'd been attacked. Somebody had chased her. Followed her to this deserted slope. Knocked her down.

And Tim had *kissed* her.

She gulped in fresh air. *Let me off this roller coaster!*

"That man." Tim's tone had gone cold, his words clipped like he was angry with her. Impersonal. He was the deputy sheriff now, on official business. "What were you thinking, heading for a deserted slope like this one with someone on your tail?"

Indignation stiffened her spine. "I didn't know he was following me." She matched his tone. "If I had, I certainly would have gone somewhere more populated."

His gaze searched hers, and then he gave a slight nod. "I didn't realize it, either. I saw you both turn into the trail, but I figured he was just cutting over to the same slope." He unzipped a pocket in his ski suit and pulled out a cell phone. "We need to report this."

"I'd rather not," she said quickly.

His eyes narrowed. "Why not?"

"Poor Mr. and Mrs. Harrison. They're worried enough as it is."

"Liz, there's a killer running loose."

She shook her head. "I'm sure this incident isn't related."

His eyes narrowed. "What makes you so sure?"

Actually, she wasn't sure. But she couldn't stand the thought of causing more problems for the Harrisons, or for Debbie. She sucked in her lower lip, then winced. The swelling had gone down after her episode with Jazzy on the chairlift, but the split was still painful. This was definitely not one of her better days.

She nodded. "You're right. Go ahead."

While he made his phone call, Liz took inventory of her aching limbs. She was going to have a bruise the size of Texas on her left hip. A throb in her right knee told her she'd wrenched it pretty good in the fall. After flexing it a couple of times, she decided the damage was minimal. She scooted across the snow toward her hat and goggles.

Tim disconnected his call and stowed his phone. "Are you hurt?"

Again, that cold tone. She risked a quick look at his face, and met a stony expression. If she hadn't just seen his feelings in his eyes, felt them in his kiss, she would think he hated her.

Judging by his reaction to her now, his feelings weren't open to discussion.

"I twisted my knee, but it's okay."

"Don't move. Help will be here soon. I told the dispatcher to notify ski patrol, as well as the sheriff."

He stood and walked across the snow to retrieve her errant ski. When he brought it back, he took her other one and stuck them both down in the snow uphill of them in the form of an X, the universally recognized signal for a downed skier. Then he stood to one side, staring uphill as though he couldn't wait for the ski patrollers to arrive and rescue him from her presence. Funny, since he'd just rescued her.

But from what? Was her attacker really the same man who shot that Jason Sinclair guy? It seemed unlikely. What possible connection could she have with a man found shot and frozen on a ski lift? Besides, her attacker didn't threaten her with a gun. More likely he was a pervert who liked to follow women to isolated areas. After all, he'd been pulling at her jacket when…

Wait. Not her jacket. Her backpack. The man had knocked her down and tried to pull off her backpack. But all she had in there was her ID, a little cash, an extra hat, a neck warmer, a leftover apple from lunch and—

A shiver worked its way down her spine.

And her grandmother's brooch.

She stole a sideways glance at Tim. She should tell him about the brooch. But he looked so distant, so cold. The last thing she wanted to do was remind him of the brooch and the reason she had it in her possession in the first place.

Besides, he'd think her a complete dope. It probably wasn't worth more than a couple hundred dollars.

At least, she didn't *think* so.

The sooner she got the thing appraised and found out for sure, the better. She'd head downtown the moment she got back to the lodge. And if she found out the thing was worth more than she thought, she'd tell Tim then.

FIFTEEN

"You're sure you don't know the man who attacked you?"

Liz had to work hard to keep from squirming under the sheriff's piercing stare. How in the world did criminals stand up to this guy? She hadn't done anything wrong, but that direct gaze made her want to find something to confess.

"As far as I know, I never saw him before in my life."

They sat in the living area of the condo, Liz with an ice pack on her knee, the sheriff and Tim seated on the sofa. Jazzy and Caitlin hovered behind them, watching wordlessly as Liz was questioned.

"As far as you know?" the sheriff probed.

Tim leaned forward and told the sheriff, "The guy was wearing a ski mask and reflective goggles. I don't think I'd have known him if he'd been my own brother."

Liz nodded. She avoided looking directly at Tim, but kept her gaze focused instead on the sheriff.

He sucked in his cheeks, which made his lips look like a fish. If the situation hadn't been so serious, Liz would have laughed.

"Did you see a gun?" Sheriff Daniels asked.

"No."

"Might he have had a gun that you didn't see?"

Liz paused. "I suppose so," she said slowly. "I mean, he

was wearing a bulky ski suit. I don't know what he had in the pockets."

"What do you think he was after, Miss Carmichael?"

Liz paused. Here's where she should say something about the brooch. But she could feel Tim's glowering presence beside the sheriff, *not* looking at her. She couldn't go into that old story right now. Besides, until she had the brooch appraised, she wouldn't know for sure if the family heirloom had anything to do with the attack or not.

She returned the sheriff's gaze. "I really don't know."

Behind him, Jazzy opened her mouth to say something, but Liz flicked a stern glance toward her and she closed it again.

Sheriff Daniels nodded, slapped his knees and stood. "Well, my men tried to trail him through the trees, but his tracks disappeared on the next ski run. My guess is the guy followed that run down to the base and left the resort with the rest of the crowd. With no identifiable gear…" He lifted a shoulder.

Tim got to his feet, as well. Liz started to pick up the ice pack so she could stand, too, but the sheriff stopped her with a raised hand.

"Sit tight, Miss Carmichael. You still have my card?" Liz nodded. "Good. Call me if you think of anything that might be helpful."

"I do have one favor to ask, Sheriff. Can we keep this quiet?" Liz cast a pleading glance toward Tim. "I don't want Debbie or Grandma to know. It will just worry them both, and they don't need that with the wedding a few days away. Please?"

The sheriff gave a single nod. "I won't say a word. You'd just better hope the press doesn't get wind of it."

Tim didn't respond one way or the other. Liz hoped he'd follow his boss's cue, though.

Caitlin walked with him and Sheriff Daniels to the door.

"Sheriff, do you think Liz is in any danger? I mean, someone was killed here the night we arrived."

The sheriff squinted, then shook his head. "I'm not saying this incident isn't related. But if it is, the circumstances point to an attacker who follows lone skiers to isolated areas of the mountain." His gaze swept all three of them. "As long as you ladies stick together, you should be fine." He dipped his head toward Liz. "Ma'am."

With that, he opened the door and left, Tim on his heels.

When the door closed behind them, Jazzy marched around the sofa and planted herself before Liz, hands on her hips. "Why didn't you tell them about your pin?"

Liz adjusted the ice pack on her knee. Jazzy and Caitlin were her best friends, certainly a safe audience to whom she could confess the tidal wave of emotions she'd felt since returning to Utah and realizing that—she swallowed—that she still loved Tim.

She wanted to tell her friends about Tim's kiss, about her certainty that he still loved her. About the consuming guilt she felt every time she thought about how she had hurt him. And how the brooch was all tied up in that guilt. But she couldn't bring herself to discuss it. Not yet.

"Because I don't know for sure that it has anything to do with all this." Caitlin started to protest, but Liz held up a hand. "Not yet, anyway. But I'm going to find out right now."

She tossed the ice bag aside and stood gingerly, testing her weight on her knee. Tender, but not bad. She took a tentative step. If she borrowed some of Jazzy's ibuprofen she'd be fine.

"Girls," she told them, "we have an important errand to run. We're going to town."

Tim pulled the door closed behind him. The sheriff paused in the hallway outside Liz's door. He stared at the closed door, his cheeks hollow as he chewed the insides.

"She's hiding something, Richards."

His tone left no hint of doubt, which confirmed Tim's instincts. The whole time he'd watched his boss question Liz, Tim had been convinced she was holding something back.

"I thought so, too." He paused, then felt compelled to defend her, at least a little. "I don't believe it's anything really important. At least, she doesn't think so. Otherwise she'd tell us."

Sheriff Daniels nodded. "Agreed. Problem is, she's not in a position to judge that. I think we need to keep an eye on her." His gaze slid sideways. "Think you can do that, Richards?"

A lump of lead dropped into Tim's stomach. The sheriff was right. Instinct told him Liz was more involved in this messy business than any of them knew—including her. For her own good, she needed someone to watch out for her. But he knew her well enough to know she would resist that suggestion with every ounce of stubborn strength she possessed. Especially if that someone turned out to be him.

Still, could he actually let the sheriff assign someone else to do surveillance on his ex-fiancée? No way.

His back straightened. "I can handle it, sir."

The sheriff's lips twitched. "No need to overdo it, Richards. Don't camp out here in the hallway or anything. Just try to make sure she doesn't get into any more trouble." The sheriff turned on his heel and marched toward the elevator.

Tim hesitated. He cast a glance at Liz's closed door. No, he wouldn't camp out in the hallway. But he had a perfect reason to stick close to her. They were both part of the wedding party, which meant they would attend the same events over the next few days.

He'd make sure she didn't go anywhere without him, starting this evening. Right after he went home to shower and change.

SIXTEEN

Liz stepped inside the jewelry store door just minutes before five o'clock, Caitlin and Jazzy on her heels. She favored her knee only a little, her limp barely noticeable. The door tone announced their presence with a high-pitched beep. The same girl who was here yesterday smiled at them from behind the glass display cases as the door swung closed behind them, cutting off the noise from Main Street.

"Can I help you?"

"Is Mr. Cole here?" Liz glanced toward the back room while Jazzy and Caitlin wandered over to one of the display cases lining the door.

"I'm afraid Mr. Cole is off today. Is there something I can do for you?"

"Can you do an appraisal?" Liz reached into her purse for the jewelry box.

The girl's face became apologetic. "I'm sorry. Mr. Cole does all the appraisals. But if you have an item you'd like to leave, I'm sure he can get to it tomorrow."

Liz hesitated. It wasn't like she was planning to wear the brooch tonight. But given the events of the past twenty-four hours, she didn't feel comfortable leaving it. She glanced at Caitlin, who gave a subtle shake of her head. Her friends agreed.

"Uh, that's okay." She dropped the box back into her purse. "We'll come back another time."

She had almost reached the front door when a male voice spoke behind her.

"Actually, I'm one of those people who can't seem to stay away from work, even on my days off. Especially when I have paperwork to do in the back office."

She turned to see Mr. Cole stepping between two display cases toward her. Recognition dawned on his features when he caught sight of her.

"Hello. Miss Carmichael, wasn't it?"

Liz nodded, relieved. He remembered her. "That's right. I was in here yesterday with my cousin."

"It's nice to see you again."

"Thank you. I'm sorry to bother you. I don't want to impose on your day off."

He smiled. "I'm at work, aren't I? I'd much rather talk to an attractive young woman than stare at inventory and cash flow reports. What can I help you with?"

Liz glanced at Jazzy and Caitlin. Where to begin?

"I overheard your conversation with Christy." He gave her an expectant look. "Something about an appraisal?"

"That's right." Liz extracted the box from her purse and extended it toward him. "I'd like to get your opinion on this."

He took a pair of glasses from his breast pocket and slipped them on before lifting the hinged lid. His eyes widened when he caught sight of the brooch inside. The fingers of his other hand moved toward it, then paused, hovering inches above the piece. He looked up at her. "May I?"

"Of course."

Gingerly, he lifted the golden pin and held it close to his face. "Beautiful workmanship. Note the bloomed gold, the subtle bends to give the appearance of ribbons. And the gems are stunning. Opals aren't known for their durability, but these are exquisite. And look at the glorious color in the emeralds. We don't see those often these days."

Liz exchanged a glance with Jazzy. The man's enthusiasm showed. His voice had taken on an almost loving tone.

He turned the piece over and examined the back side. "Ah. See these loops here?"

Liz looked at the golden circles above the pin's shaft. "I've noticed them before. Are they for a chain?"

"Exactly. This piece could be worn either as a brooch or a pendant. Ladies of that era sometimes preferred not to pierce the silk of their gowns."

Caitlin stepped forward to peer at the brooch. "What era would that be?"

"Off the top of my head I'd say early 1800s. And British." He held the brooch closer to his eyes and squinted. "Yes, I was right. Definitely British."

"Really?" Liz looked at the pin with a touch of consternation. She'd known it was at least a hundred years old because of the picture Grandma showed her when she was a child. Mr. Cole put the age at almost twice that. If she'd known, she wouldn't have dared to wear it at all. "Are you sure?"

Mr. Cole gave her a brief smile. "My dear, that's what I do. Here. Take a look at this."

He pulled a ballpoint pen out of his pocket and pointed with the capped end toward a small emblem etched into the gold on the back, beneath the pin shaft.

"It looks like a code of some sort," Liz said.

"Exactly. It's called 'hallmarking.' Each symbol represents something. The first is the maker's mark, typically his initials, as here with the AB. The others indicate the assay office and the standard mark, which denotes the quality of the gold. Sometimes you'll also find a date letter and a duty mark. Unfortunately, this piece doesn't have those. They would be most helpful in pinpointing the exact age."

"This is just like *Antiques Roadshow!*" Jazzy rubbed her hands together, clearly delighted. "How much is it worth?"

Mr. Cole considered. "Of course, I can't be exact without tracing the hallmark, but…" He turned the piece back over to look at the front. "I'd say between twelve and fifteen."

The numbers seeped into Liz's brain. He couldn't mean fifteen dollars. The gold content itself would be worth more than that. Which meant he was saying Grandma's brooch was worth—

"Fifteen *hundred* dollars?" Caitlin gasped.

Liz felt lightheaded. She'd been carrying fifteen hundred dollars worth of jewelry around with her for the past three years. In her jewelry box at home. Pinned to her performance clothes when she played at weddings. She gulped. In her backpack on the slopes today.

"As I said, I'd have to check to be sure of an exact price. It may be less." He set the pin back in the box and admired it on its velvet bed. "But if you're in the market to sell, I'll give you fifteen hundred right now for it."

Liz gasped. "I can't sell it! It's a family heirloom. My grandmother would kill me."

A smile played at the corners of his mouth. "Yes, she's a formidable woman. And quite the bargainer." He closed the lid with care. "If you'll leave it with me tonight, I can have an exact figure for you in the morning, along with the appraisal certificate."

Discomfort tickled at the edges of Liz's mind. No doubt he'd take good care of the brooch. And she really didn't feel safe carrying the thing around, especially after what happened today on the slopes. Still, something didn't feel right about leaving it.

She held out her hand, palm up. "If it's all the same to you, I'd prefer not."

Mr. Cole paused, and she wondered if she had offended

him. Then he gave a nod. He started to place the box in her hand, but hesitated. "Would you mind if I took some pictures? It will help me in my research tonight. And we'll need them for the appraisal certificate anyway."

"Of course."

"I'll get my camera from the back office."

He made as if to walk away, but Liz kept her hand extended. With a brief smile, he relinquished the box.

Liz's fingers curled around the velvet. Now that she knew the value, she wasn't about to let this thing out of her sight until she figured out what to do with it.

Tim sank into a suede chair in the lobby of the lodge. He couldn't see the elevator, but he could watch the corner that Liz and her friends would have to come around when they rode down to the main floor.

He ran a hand through his still-damp hair. The heat from the fire blazing in the grate felt good on his freezing-cold head. He'd been too anxious to take the time to dry it after his shower. He'd thrown on his clothes and headed over here, afraid Liz and the others might leave to go shopping or something while he was gone.

"Don't camp out in the hallway," the sheriff had instructed. Okay, the lobby wasn't the hallway. He could sit here and read the newspaper or something, and look completely normal.

Newspaper! No newspaper nearby, but he leaned forward and grabbed a magazine from those scattered on the surface of the coffee table. He leaned against the rear cushion, crossed his leg and propped the magazine open in front of him. There. Now he looked normal, and he could see over the top.

The lobby was deserted except for the dark-haired woman named Kate sitting behind the front desk. After a curious glance his way, she ignored him.

He waited. Liz and the others would have to come down sooner or later to go get something to eat. Unless they were planning to cook in their room, but he didn't think they'd do that. Or maybe they'd order a pizza or something, and he'd see the delivery guy—

Tim sat straight up. Pizza! Tonight was the bachelor party he and the other guys were throwing for Ryan. He'd totally forgotten. They were planning to order pizza and play video games on the two television sets up in Ryan's condo. And later on, a girl from Tim's church was going to deliver a singing telegram. Nothing risqué, just a pretty Christian girl who would do a little good-natured kidding of the groom.

Relief made him smile as he remembered the girls had similar plans. They were going to hang out in Debbie's room and have a pajama party or something. Which meant Liz wouldn't be going anywhere tonight. She'd stay right here, safely surrounded by a whole passel of women.

He glanced at his watch. Just past five-thirty. He and the other guys weren't supposed to be up in Ryan's room until seven. He relaxed again in the chair. Plenty of time for him to run home and grab the Nintendo Wii games he'd promised to bring to play on Patrick's machine. If only he could think of a valid excuse to call Liz, make sure she planned to stay in her condo until their party started.

The main entrance doors swung open. Tim glanced that way casually, and then his head jerked sideways when he caught sight of the group that entered the lobby. He came to his feet.

"Liz!"

She turned toward him. "Tim?"

"Where have you been?" He covered the space between them with determined steps to stand before her. "I thought you were upstairs in your room."

Her eyebrows climbed up her forehead toward her bangs as she looked up into his face.

Obviously, he was coming on a little too strong. "Uh, I mean, you need to keep some ice on that knee. You twisted it pretty good." *How lame was that?* He hid a cringe.

She answered with a polite smile. "My knee is fine. What are you doing here?"

What am I doing here? He cast around for a plausible explanation.

"Reading a magazine while I wait for Ryan." He held the proof up for her inspection.

Liz's friends stood beside her, each of them trying to hide grins. Unsuccessfully.

The blonde, Caitlin, nodded toward his magazine. "Do you read *Women's Day* often?"

Tim glanced down at the magazine. Bummer. He hadn't even noticed. He met her gaze and answered evenly, "It has some very good articles."

A smile twitched at the girl's lips. "Yes, it does."

The ski klutz, Jazzy, stepped toward him. "Actually, it's a good thing you're here. Liz has something to tell you." She gave Liz a stern look. "Don't you, Liz?"

"Uh, well." Liz's gaze slid from one of her friends to the other. She blew out a sigh that might have been resignation. "Yes, I guess I do. Let's go sit down. This might take a minute."

She reached for the purse hanging from her shoulder.

The front door whooshed open again, letting in a blast of cold air. Tim looked up—

—and into the last face he wanted to see.

Jeremy Norville was here.

"Liz! What a surprise."

Tim's teeth clenched as he watched the guy embrace Liz with a hug. No kiss this time, thank goodness. What was his former friend and all-time jerk doing here? Surely Ryan wouldn't invite him to their gaming party.

"Jeremy." The smile Liz turned on the guy seemed genuine. Jealousy churned in Tim's gut. She didn't smile at *him* like that. "I wasn't sure I'd see you again before I leave to go back to Kentucky."

"Well, I couldn't let that happen, could I?" Norville widened that smirk of his to include the other women. Naturally. "And who do we have here?"

"These are my friends from Kentucky."

Tim stood to one side, his insides boiling, and tried to keep his expression calm as Liz introduced her friends and explained to Norville about their musical trio. It was all he could do not to sock the guy and knock out a few of those white teeth he appeared to be so proud of. He sure flashed them around a lot.

"So what are you really doing here, Jeremy?" Liz asked. "Are you hanging out with Ryan and the guys tonight?"

Norville's glance slid toward Tim for an instant. "No, I'm here to pick up my date." He flashed a grimace of apology toward Liz. "Sorry, Lizzie. Uh—" He held his palms up. "I mean, Liz."

Tim felt a rush of relief at the news. Norville had a date. Good. He knew he wasn't up for an evening spent in the guy's annoying presence. But Tim noticed Liz didn't seem relieved.

"A date?" Her smile became polite.

Was she jealous? Tim swallowed, his throat thick.

"Yeah. Kate and I've been going out a couple of months." The guy dipped his head toward the front desk, where the dark-haired woman stood watching them.

Tim felt his jaw go slack. She had to be at least ten years older than Norville. Not that she was unattractive, just…old. Or *older,* anyway. Late thirties, if he was any judge.

"Yeah, I know it's a little weird." Norville lowered his voice, his eyes on Kate. "But she's really nice, and we get along. And she's mature, you know? It's about time I started thinking about serious stuff, like saving money and setting career goals, maybe starting a family someday."

Tim wanted to snort, but held it back at the last moment. Norville growing up? Not a chance.

"I'm…glad for you, Jeremy. I hope it works out."

Liz's smile looked forced. And he'd heard hesitation in her voice. Was she jealous? Did she still have feelings for the guy?

The thought wedged in Tim's brain like ice. What was he doing standing here, listening to this garbage? He turned on his heel and headed toward the fireplace to return the magazine. He'd leave. Call the sheriff and tell him to assign someone else to keep an eye on Liz. He couldn't handle this.

SEVENTEEN

Liz started when Tim turned abruptly and stomped away. Jeremy stared after him a moment, then gave a slight shrug. Jazzy and Caitlin both wore inquisitive expressions as their gazes slid between the two men. They were probably picking up on the unspoken nuances.

"Listen, Jeremy," Liz said, "I need to talk to Tim about something before he leaves. Will I see you again? At the wedding, maybe?"

Jeremy watched Tim's retreating back for a moment. Then he shook his head. "I don't think so. Best not to rub it in, you know? Apparently some of us haven't moved on in three years."

Irritation stabbed through Liz at his slightly superior tone. He had no right—zero—to feel superior to Tim. She straightened her spine and jumped to Tim's defense. "Well, maybe some wounds take a little longer to heal. The deep ones."

Jazzy and Caitlin's expressions were more than inquisitive now. They were downright curious. Liz had confessed about her engagement to Tim last night before dinner, but she hadn't included Jeremy in the explanation. Obviously, she was going to have some explaining to do later.

"Whatever." He shrugged again. "Listen, it was nice to

meet you two." He nodded at her friends, then threw an arm around Liz for a quick hug. "Keep in touch, okay?"

"I will."

He headed for the front desk and his date. Which was beyond weird, as far as Liz was concerned. That Jeremy Norville would actually go for a woman who looked to be in her late thirties just about blew her mind. Nothing against Kate, who seemed nice enough, but she didn't fit the mold for Jeremy's typical girlfriend. She was slightly on the heavy side, for one, and short. And she didn't look at all like a powder hound, as Jeremy had always been.

But hey, people could change, couldn't they? Maybe Jeremy really had grown up.

Tim had tossed his magazine on the surface of the coffee table and was heading toward the door. One glance at his stormy expression made Liz want to forget the whole thing. She had the sheriff's business card. Maybe she could just give him a call.

But Caitlin apparently wasn't going to let this opportunity pass. She stepped into Tim's path to stop him. "Where are you going? We told you, Liz needs to talk to you."

"That's right." Jazzy nodded. "Don't you, Liz?"

Tim turned an expectant stare her way. Liz sucked in a breath. "Yeah. I guess I do."

He paused, his eyes flickering toward the door. *He's contemplating his exit!* Liz was just about to draw an outraged breath and tell him to go ahead and leave when he allowed a smile to flash onto his face.

"All right. Let's have a seat."

Liz followed him back toward the fireplace. He returned to the chair he'd been sitting in when they arrived earlier, and she sat on the couch nearest to him. Jazzy and Caitlin dropped onto the cushions beside her.

She gave them a look. "Don't you have somewhere to be? Practicing our music, maybe?"

They both gave her guileless smiles.

"We can't practice without our cellist," Caitlin said.

Jazzy nodded. "Besides, we want to make sure you don't leave anything out."

Liz rolled her eyes at them. "Fine." She turned toward Tim. "I think I might know what that man was after on the slopes today."

Tim sucked in a slow breath. "What?"

"This." Liz reached into her purse and pulled out the box. She held it in her palm for a moment. Tim would recognize it immediately, of course. And the memories associated with the thing wouldn't be pleasant ones for him. But she had to show him. She thrust the box into his hands.

A cautious expression stole over his features as he searched her face. Then he opened the lid as gently as Mr. Cole had done earlier. Liz watched him carefully for a reaction, but all she saw was his throat move once as he swallowed.

"Your family heirloom." His voice was flat, devoid of any emotion. "You still have it."

"Grandma didn't want to take it back after…what happened." She cleared her throat. "I'm supposed to give it to Debbie on Saturday."

Tim shook his head. "Let me get this straight. You had this with you on the slopes today?"

She nodded. "In my backpack."

"Why would you carry it with you while you skied?"

"Because I was afraid someone might break into our hotel room and steal it."

His gaze rose from the pin to Liz's face. "Why would you think that?"

Liz clasped her hands between her knees and looked down at them.

Caitlin answered for her. "Because we think someone

searched our condo yesterday while we were out. And Debbie thought someone might have been in hers, too."

"Not only that," Jazzy said, "but six weeks ago Liz's apartment was broken into back in Kentucky. Whoever it was trashed the place, but they didn't steal anything."

"We think they might have been looking for the pin, which Liz had with her that night," Caitlin added.

Disbelief grew stronger on Tim's face with each word. "Liz, why didn't you tell me this before? Why didn't you tell the sheriff this afternoon?"

She grasped her hands more tightly. Time for full disclosure, even though it might be painful. "Because I didn't want to remind you of the reason I have the heirloom to begin with. I was embarrassed."

Apparently Jazzy and Caitlin felt they'd served their purpose. They rose and slipped away without a word. Liz didn't look at them as they left.

"Elizabeth Ann Carmichael."

Liz's head rose almost of its own accord in response to the tenderness in Tim's voice. His eyes, light brown with flecks of green in patterns she had memorized long ago, reflected his tone. Alarm claxons sounded in her mind. *Danger! Danger! Don't go there.* But her lips tingled with the memory of his kiss on the slopes.

"No embarrassment between us," he whispered. "We've been through too much for that."

Liz felt herself slipping over the edge of a precipice. If she leaned forward a tiny bit, gave him the slightest encouragement, he would kiss her again. She knew it. But did she really want it? Okay, yes. She wanted to lose herself in his kiss the way she used to, back before the whole mess with Jeremy had destroyed their lives. But the past was full of guilt and pain—the pain she'd inflicted on Tim and on herself. This was dangerous emotional ground, and she wasn't sure she could handle it. She had to get a grip on herself, on the situation.

She straightened her spine, which made her lean backward, out of the danger zone. "I just didn't want to make you uncomfortable, that's all. Especially in front of your boss."

Tim held her gaze for a long moment, then gave a nearly imperceptible nod. He leaned back in his chair, as well, and closed the lid on the box.

"Did you or Debbie tell anyone about your room being searched yesterday?"

Her muscles relaxed at the normal tone he used. "No. We weren't even positive anyone had been there. I'm still not sure. If someone did search our room, they were very careful not to leave any signs."

He held the jewelry box up. "You know I'll have to report this to Sheriff Daniels?"

Liz nodded. She'd probably have to answer some tough questions, like why she chose to keep this from him before. "Honestly, it didn't occur to me at first that the guy on the mountain would want my grandmother's brooch. I mean, nobody knows about it except my family. Plus, I didn't think it was worth much until about an hour ago."

Tim's eyebrows rose. "Oh?"

Liz told him about their visit to the jewelry store and Mr. Cole's estimation of the value of the pin.

"Even so," she concluded, "I still don't see how my apartment getting trashed back in December could have anything to do with today. It just doesn't make sense."

Tim pursed his lips and stared at the velvet box. "It does seem unlikely. But we have to check it out anyway. The sheriff will probably contact the police in Kentucky for a copy of their report. If there's a connection, we'll figure it out. In the meantime, we need to put this someplace safe."

Liz agreed wholeheartedly. "Do you have a safe-deposit box?"

"Yeah, but the bank is closed for the night." He glanced behind her, toward the front desk. "How about the lodge's safe?"

Liz looked over her shoulder. Thank goodness Jeremy and his girlfriend had left. Mr. Harrison sat behind the desk, his head bent over his hands as he wrote something. "Perfect."

Tim nodded and stood. "And one other thing. I want you to stay here tonight. Hang out with your friends and Debbie and your grandmother. I'll be right here in the lodge, in Ryan's room with the guys. If you do have to go anywhere, you call me and I'll go with you, okay?"

Liz bristled. "I don't need a bodyguard."

"I knew you'd say that." Tim grinned. "Some things never change."

Something inside Liz melted as she returned that oh-so-familiar grin. He was right. Some things never changed, no matter how far she ran. Even all the way to Kentucky.

EIGHTEEN

After he'd seen Liz safely to her room—with her protesting the need for an escort all the way—Tim slipped out his cell phone and punched in the number for the sheriff. As he waited for the call to connect, Tim walked toward the stairwell at the end of the hall. Ryan's room was at the other end of the building and one floor down. Far enough away to make Liz feel that he wasn't hovering over her, but close enough that he could get to her quickly if he needed to. He planned to crash on the floor in Ryan's condo tonight, since that one had only a single bedroom and the other guys planned to stay over. Tim *could* go back to his apartment for the night. But he felt better sticking close to Liz.

The phone didn't complete the first ring when it was answered.

"Daniels."

"Sheriff, it's Tim Richards. I need to report a development in the Eagle Summit case." He laid out the pertinent information about the brooch and Liz's suspicions that her room had been searched in succinct details.

Daniels remained silent until he had finished. "What about the cleaning crew? Any chance they were in her room?"

"No, sir. I checked with the resort owner when we locked the pin in his safe, and he said no cleaning crew had been up there yesterday. They only clean the condos once each week, and between guests."

Harrison had been horrified at the suggestion that someone had gone through his guests' rooms. He insisted that all the room keys were kept secured. Tim glanced at the door he passed. Standard, if old-fashioned, locking handle and dead bolt.

The sheriff let out a disgusted blast. "Why didn't the Carmichael girl tell us this afternoon?"

Tim gulped. He really didn't want to go into their whole background in front of his boss. "It was me, sir. As I told you this morning, we have a history."

"Do I need to pull you out of there?"

"No, sir." He reached the stairwell and stood with his hand on the door handle. "I just left Miss Carmichael, and we've gotten past it."

Well, maybe not all the way past it, but at least Liz had opened up to him. About the pin, anyway.

"Oh, and one other thing, sheriff." Tim described the break-in at Liz's apartment six weeks ago. "Hard to see how that's related, but I thought you might want to have someone follow up on it."

"Good job, Richards. I'm going to send a couple of deputies over there to hang around that lodge, keep an eye on the place. Act as a deterrent. You got things under control with the girl?"

Tim scuffed his shoe against the carpet in the hallway. "Well, I'm trying. She got away from me this afternoon. But at least she was with her friends. And I've got her promise she won't leave the lodge alone without letting me know."

"Ha!" The sheriff's laugh spoke volumes about what he thought of Liz's promise. "Still, maybe she's scared enough now to listen to reason. All right, Richards. I'll need some paperwork from you by tomorrow. Lay it all out. In the meantime, I'll have someone contact the police in…" Tim heard a paper rattle in the background "…Lexington, Kentucky. You don't have the exact date of that break-in, do you?"

"No, just December. Want me to ask her?" Tim half-turned to head back down the hallway to Liz's room.

"Nah, they can figure it out."

Sheriff Daniels ended the call without another word. Tim gave a silent laugh and slid the phone into his pocket. Apparently his boss didn't waste breath on unnecessary things like saying goodbye.

He'd taken a few steps down the hall when his cell phone rang. The ring tone echoed in the hollow stairwell. Tim fished it out as he walked and glanced at the screen.

"Hey, Mom," he said as he rounded the landing.

"Hi, honey. I'm not bothering you, am I?" His mother's voice held the slightly anxious tone it always did when she was afraid she was interrupting him.

"No, I'm just on my way to Ryan's room for the bachelor party."

"You're not going to be drinking, are you?" Her tone changed to stern disapproval.

Tim laughed. "Mom, you know better than that."

"Sorry. You always were a good boy, even as a teenager. Unlike your sister."

"Hey, I heard that!"

The sound of Maggie's outraged comment in the background made him smile.

Mom chuckled in his ear. "Listen, I called to ask you something. At church last night I heard that Liz Carmichael is in town for her cousin's wedding."

Tim almost missed a step. "Yes, ma'am. She is."

"Have you seen her?"

"A couple of times. Just a few minutes ago, in fact."

Mom's voice warmed. "Oh, Tim, please tell her I said hello, and that I've missed her so much."

Tim snapped his mouth shut. Mom had always loved Liz, and had been almost as devastated over their broken engagement as him.

"Mother!" Maggie's voice sounded closer. "I cannot believe you just asked Tim to talk to that woman. That's like tossing your own flesh and blood into a rattlesnake pit. She broke his heart, or have you forgotten that?"

Mom sounded immediately contrite. "Well, if it will make you uncomfortable, of course you don't have to relay my message."

"No, it's okay." Tim reached the next floor and swung open the fire door. "I'll probably see her again tomorrow. I'll tell her you said hello."

"Thank you, honey."

"Here, let me talk to him," Maggie snapped. Tim winced and jerked the phone away as Maggie's voice blared into his ear. "Don't you dare talk to her! In fact, stay as far away from her as you can. I don't know what Ryan was thinking, asking you to be in his wedding when he knew she would be around. Some best friend he turned out to be."

"Calm down, Sis." Tim pictured his pregnant sister, face red with righteous indignation at the thought of her brother being insulted. "It's not good for you to get all hyper. Think of the kid."

That always calmed her down. He heard her huff a few breaths of oxygen. "I'm perfectly calm. I'm just worried about my baby brother." Her voice lowered to almost a whisper. "So, have you seen her yet?"

"Yes, several times."

"Was it, you know, okay?"

Tim detected real concern in her question, and felt a rush of warmth for his big sister. She'd always been protective of him. "It was fine. Really. She looks good."

"Oh, no, you did not just say that."

"What? She's not allowed to look good?"

"That is not what you said. Oh, those were the words, but that's not what you meant." Her words became a hiss. "You're still in love with her, aren't you? You saw her and did a back flip and ended up falling right at her feet, didn't you?"

Tim stopped in the hallway and leaned against the wall, eyes closed. Maggie had always possessed the uncanny ability to pick up on his thoughts, no matter how he tried to hide them from her. That kiss on the slopes today had felt just like that, a backflip. He kept his voice carefully bland. "I did not."

"There it is again," she accused. "I hear it in your voice. Please tell me you haven't done anything stupid, like tell her you're still in love with her."

"Of course not."

"But?"

Tim remembered the look that passed between them downstairs. He'd seen something in Liz's eyes that made him wonder if she might still have feelings for him. Hope lifted his mood to the roof at the thought.

Still, he wasn't about to discuss that with his sister.

"But nothing," he said.

"Good. Because if you're tempted, you just remember how awful you felt when she dumped you. How you wouldn't leave my apartment for days. How your stomach was so sick you couldn't eat."

"Okay, okay. I remember." Tim hefted himself off the wall. "Listen, I've got to go. Tonight's the bachelor party."

"I'm not kidding, Tim. Don't set yourself up again. If I have to come up there and knock you around, I'll do it."

Tim couldn't help smiling at the visual image that threat caused. "I'd like to see you try. Love you, Sis."

"Love you, too, Little Brother."

In the background he heard Mom shout, "Tell him to be sure and wear his bulletproof vest when he's working."

He laughed. "Tell her I always do. Bye."

Tim shook his head as he disconnected the call. Maggie had never given up her role of Big Sister Protector, and truth be told, he wouldn't have her any other way. Besides, she was right—the pain when Liz dumped him for Jeremy had been almost more than he could bear. But the memory of pain faded in the light of hope, and Tim couldn't stop thinking about the way Liz had melted in his arms when he'd kissed her on the slopes. Maybe she wasn't still in love with him… but maybe she was. If he had a chance, even a slim one, of getting her back, he was willing to take the risk of being hurt again. No matter what Maggie said.

Liz closed the door behind her and threw the dead bolt. Seconds later, Jazzy and Caitlin charged out of their bedroom. They took up stances in front of her.

"Okay, girl, truth time." Jazzy planted her hands on her hips and glared into Liz's face. "You've been holding out on us."

Caitlin agreed. "Yeah. Who is this Jeremy character, and what is the deal between him and Tim? And *you?*"

Liz heaved a sigh. "Truth time" indeed. And right now her head was spinning so much she needed to talk it out. What better listeners than her best friends?

"Okay, I'm ready to come clean."

She allowed herself to be guided to the couch. Jazzy sat beside her, and Caitlin perched on the matching chair. They turned expectant gazes her way, two invitations to spill her guts. No, not invitations. Those expressions were too insistent to be called anything less than demands.

"Okay, what I told you last night about Tim was absolutely true. But I didn't tell you the whole story about how we broke up."

Jazzy snorted. "No kidding."

Caitlin gave her a stern glare. "Go ahead, Liz."

Liz drew in a breath. "After our engagement, I started feeling…I don't know. Trapped." She stared at her hands in her lap. "Marriage is a permanent step. And I kept wondering if I was making a mistake."

"Didn't you love him?" Caitlin's voice was soft.

Liz sucked in her lower lip. "Ye-es." She said it like a confession. And maybe it was. "I did. But I started wondering if love is enough, you know? Tim and I went to a church down in the valley. There was a couple we got really close to. They kind of took us under their wing, you know? We went out to dinner together, and played games at their apartment almost every weekend. They'd been married five years and I really looked up to them. I guess they were having problems we didn't know about, because they got divorced right after Tim and I announced our engagement. It threw me. I mean, if it could happen to them, what made me think Tim and I would make it?"

She paused, then let out a humorless laugh. "You have to understand, I didn't lay out my thoughts logically at the time. It's only been recently that I've put all my feelings together. But I see now that their divorce really sent me into a tailspin."

The next part was hard to admit. Liz couldn't meet either of her friends' gazes. "Jeremy was one of Tim's friends. They've known each other since high school, and we all ran around together during college. He worked with Tim and Ryan as a lift operator on weekends during ski season. Jeremy's always been a big flirt. I guess I just let the flirting go too far."

"How far did it go?" Jazzy's tone held a surprising amount of compassion.

Heat burned in Liz's face. She could not lift her gaze from the carpet in front of her feet. "We were in the commons at the U. We'd had finals that day. Jeremy and I took an English lit class together, and we'd left class after the exam to get a cup of coffee. We picked out a quiet bench to recover, you know? Just sit in the sun and let the strain of the exam seep out. One thing led to another and he kissed me. And then he kissed me again. And I responded. Several times." Liz closed her eyes. She couldn't stand to remember what had happened next. "That's how Tim found us."

"Ouch," Jazzy said.

"Oh, poor Tim." Caitlin's voice held a trace of the pain Liz felt at the memory. "He must have been devastated."

Liz nodded, miserable at the vivid memory of Tim's face. "He was. But even worse, over the next few days I decided if I could respond to Jeremy like that, I couldn't really love Tim as much as I thought I did. So I broke off our engagement." She gave a silent laugh. "Not that he wouldn't have broken up with me if I hadn't done it first. I didn't even face him to give him his ring back. I made Debbie do it."

Caitlin leaned back in the chair. "Well, that explains why Tim is so hostile to Jeremy."

"Yeah," Jazzy agreed, "but what about you and Jeremy? What happened there? There don't seem to be any hard feelings between you two."

"Oh, trust me, there were." Liz bounced off the couch and paced over to the silent television. "We had a fling for about a month after Tim and I broke up." Two sets of eyebrows arched. "Not that kind of fling," she hurried to say. "But I admit I thought he might be future husband material. Until he dumped me."

Her friends winced.

"That must have hurt," Jazzy said.

Liz nodded. "I've been nursing a grudge against him for three years, until we ran into him at the Java Hut last night. That's when I realized I wasn't really angry with Jeremy."

"Let me guess." Caitlin's smile bore so much sympathy Liz's eyes filled with tears. "You were angry with yourself."

Liz nodded. "Jeremy shares some of the guilt, but I can't do anything about that. The only person I can answer for is myself. And you want to know a secret?"

Jazzy slapped a hand to her chest. "There's more? I don't know if my heart can take it."

Liz smiled through tear-flooded eyes at Jazzy's dramatics. She cleared her throat and blinked to clear her vision. She did not cry easily, and she hated it when she did.

"I think Tim still has feelings for me."

Her friends exchanged tiny smiles.

"Yeah," Caitlin said, "so what's the secret?"

Liz stared at the two of them.

"Oh, come on, Liz." Jazzy shook her head. "Are you going to tell us you haven't noticed him watching you? He can't keep his eyes off you."

"Yeah, but he's always glaring at me. Like he hates me or something. Not that I'd blame him." One traitorous tear slid down her right cheek. Liz brushed it away with an impatient gesture.

Caitlin leaned forward, watching Liz carefully. "Is it possible you don't know that you're still in love with the guy?"

Liz's head shot up. "I am not!"

Jazzy laughed. "Oh, Liz. Who are you kidding? You're talking to *us*. Your friends."

Liz returned their stares with a defiant one of her own. For about five seconds. Then the enormity of what they were saying broke over her. She bowed her head and covered her face with her hands. "I can't love him. I can't! Things can never be the same between us. You don't understand what I put him through."

Her own sobs sounded loud in her ears, gut-wrenching moans from the depths of her guilty heart. She felt two pairs of arms surround her, and she buried her face in someone's shoulder.

"Come on." Caitlin's even tone broke into her grief and Liz felt herself being pulled toward the couch. "It's time to pray about this."

Liz realized her friend was right. It was long past time to pray.

NINETEEN

An unfamiliar sound echoed through the jewelry store just as he was getting ready to close the doors for the night.

Christy paused in the act of pulling on her coat to glance at him. "Mr. Cole, I think your cell phone is ringing in the office."

Duke Cole's grip on the door handle tightened. His personal cell phone had a different ring tone. This was one he didn't hear often. The fact that it was ringing now didn't portend good news.

He forced a calm smile. "So it is. If you'll let yourself out, I'll go grab it."

Christy selected a key from her key ring and held it up with a smile. "Sure thing. Have a good night."

The door tone sounded as Christy left the store. He heard her key turning in the lock from the outside as he hurried through the showroom and into the office.

The untraceable cell phone, the cheap prepaid kind, had been purchased by Jason Sinclair in Lexington, Kentucky, on Duke's orders. With Jason gone, only two people had the number. One was his associate in the brooch deal. The other…

Duke grabbed his jacket off the hook on the office wall and fished the phone out of the inside pocket. A glance at the screen showed him the number was not local. His pulse performed a queer rhumba as he pressed the talk button.

Keep the voice pleasant. Calm. He'll be able to tell if you're nervous.

"Yes?"

"Do you have it?" English, but the heavy accent made the words difficult to understand.

"Not yet. But I've seen it."

"It is genuine?"

Duke closed his eyes. An image of the lovely piece swam into focus. "Without a doubt."

"But you don't have it." The hint of an edge crept into the man's voice. "Six weeks, and you still don't have it."

He gulped. *Steady, steady. Sound confident.* "I have pictures I can send you."

"Pictures are worth nothing."

"They're proof. It's within reach. I've seen it, held it. I'll have it within a few days."

A long pause. "Very well. Send your pictures."

Duke's head went light with relief. "I'll e-mail them tonight. You'll be very happy with the piece."

"If you deliver the Jersey Brooch you will make a good addition to our organization." The accented voice broke the last word into separate syllables. "Of course, if you do not…" The man's tone sounded pleasant. Almost as though he would enjoy the consequences if Duke couldn't get the brooch.

Duke swallowed. Hard. "I will deliver."

"Good. Oh, one more thing. There has been a change of plans. You will turn over the brooch in person. I will pick it up from your store on Saturday."

Duke sank into the desk chair. The big boss was coming here? Why? They had a perfectly good delivery plan that didn't require anyone coming into the jewelry store. What if someone saw him, noted his presence? "Are you sure that's wise? What if you're seen?"

A low laugh purred through the phone. "I am very careful."

Duke didn't dare speak. He didn't trust his voice.

"Send your pictures. I will contact you on Saturday."

The phone went dead.

A dozen clocks ticked in the other room like drumbeats in the silence. The rhythm of Duke's racing heartbeat jangled in contrast to their even pulses. He *had* to get that brooch. The Carmichael girl would be back tomorrow to pick up her appraisal. With luck, she would bring the piece with her. If he could manage to get it into the back room, or even behind a counter for a minute, he could pull a switch.

Of course, he'd need a substitute. And he didn't have one. A decent forgery would take months to produce. The workmanship in the gold, the quality of the gemstones, all those things took time to pull together. And he only had one night. He glanced at his watch. Thirteen hours before the store opened at ten tomorrow.

But first he had to e-mail the pictures. And he couldn't do it from here. The university library down in the valley was open until midnight. He'd have to send them from one of the computers there. That way they couldn't be traced to him if things turned nasty.

Duke dropped his head into his hands. The way the situation looked tonight, things could become very nasty, indeed.

TWENTY

"Dude! You just wiped out my truck."

Patrick's fist connected with Tim's shoulder, but Tim didn't relax his grip on the Nintendo Wii remote, even though the energetic music Ryan had customized for this video game vibrated in his ears. Good thing the condos around them were empty, or they might get reported for disturbing the peace.

He jerked the device sideways. The truck on the television screen in front of him responded by rounding a sharp corner on two wheels. A gigantic rock loomed ahead of him in the center of the dirt road. Tim swayed sideways, his red monster truck matching the motion of his controller. At exactly the right moment, he mashed the 2 button and watched the truck return to the road.

"Whoa, that was close," Ryan said.

Out of the corner of his eye, Tim saw him lean forward to grab a handful of chips from the bag on the coffee table. Patrick dropped to the couch, leaving the space in front of the television free for Tim to maneuver. He stepped sideways to position himself dead center in front of the Nintendo Wii console.

Tim's cell phone rang. "Aw, not now! I'm almost to the finish."

"Let it go, dude." Ryan stuffed a stack of chips into his mouth and chomped. "They'll call back."

Tim was tempted. But what if it was Liz calling to say she needed to go somewhere? He wouldn't put it past her to leave the lodge without him, even though she'd promised to let him know. Her voice mocked him in his head. "Hey, I tried to call. You didn't answer."

Tim puffed a blast of air. "Can't. Patrick, bring 'er in for me."

Patrick jumped up and took the remote Tim thrust toward him. He stepped into Tim's place in the center of the room as Tim jogged to the dinette table and grabbed his phone. The display showed a local number. He punched the talk button as he made his way to the bedroom, away from the loud music.

"This is Tim Richards."

"Daniels here." The sheriff paused. "Richards, what is that racket?"

Tim closed the door and the music dimmed considerably. "Uh, I'm just hanging with some friends, Sheriff." A glance at the alarm clock on the nightstand between the two beds showed him the time was after ten o'clock. *Uh-oh.* Must be something major for Sheriff Daniels to call him this late. "Has something happened?"

"The boys dug up a piece of evidence I thought you'd want to be aware of. Remember our murder vic, Jason Sinclair? Seems he took a trip last December. You'll never guess where."

"Kentucky?"

"Bingo. Guy wasn't too smart, apparently. He bought his plane ticket with cash, but flew under his own name. Rented a car with his Visa card. Stayed in a Days Inn registered in his name, paid for with the same card. He was there for two days, but kept a low profile. Didn't cause any trouble for the local PD."

Tim's free hand tightened into a fist. "Except for when he broke into Liz's apartment and trashed the place."

"It appears that way. Safe to say he was after that fancy pin she showed you."

Tim paced to the window, thoughts piling up one after another. "Did Sinclair have any priors?"

"Couple of B and E charges, but no convictions. And those were local."

"Why Liz's heirloom pin?" Tim pulled the curtain back from the window and stared into the darkness outside without seeing. "Were the prior B and E charges connected to missing jewelry?"

"Not really. I had the boys pull the reports. A few minor rings and necklaces, nothing antique. Electronics mostly, and cash. Guy liked to gamble, according to his credit card statements. Spent a lot of time in Wendover, with a few recent trips down to Vegas. No legitimate job on record, though his mother says she gave him money on a regular basis, told her he was paid under the table laying flooring for a guy. I'll eat yellow snow if he ever laid flooring. My instinct tells me Sinclair was a local thug working for somebody else."

Tim nodded. Logical conclusion. "Somebody who decided they didn't need him around anymore."

"That's right." The sheriff paused. "Richards, you know what this means, don't you?"

Ice settled in Tim's core. No doubt now that the murder and the attack on Liz were connected. "There's a killer running around. And he's after Liz's pin."

"I don't think she ought to keep that thing on her."

"She isn't. It's secure."

"Good. I've stepped up patrol in the Eagle Summit area, and don't forget there are a couple of deputies hanging out there tonight. You make sure that girl understands the situation so she doesn't go off and do something stupid, you hear?"

Tim straightened. The sheriff barely knew Liz at all, but apparently he'd picked up on her stubborn streak. "Is it okay to tell her what you dug up?"

"Yeah. Maybe it'll convince her to take precautions."

A dull silence followed Sheriff Daniels's statement. Tim looked at the display. "Call Ended." He shook his head. The guy really had a thing against saying goodbye.

"Oh, Liz, thank you! It's just beautiful." Debbie lifted the white nightie Liz had bought for her out of the tissue paper and held it up for everyone to see. "Isn't it stunning? I'm going to wear this on my wedding night."

Liz could have looked at the light shining in her cousin's eyes all night. Back when she was in school, she'd had an abstract art teacher who'd given them assignments to paint emotions, like sadness, or joy. If Liz had to paint happy right now, she'd use Debbie as a model.

Grandma leaned forward to pick up a carrot stick from the veggie tray on the coffee table. Liz caught the smile hovering at the edges of her mouth. Grandma was thoroughly enjoying this bachelorette party. No doubt it had been a long time since she'd been included as "one of the girls."

Someone pounded on the door. Betsy was closest, so she got up and put an eye to the peephole. She addressed the room. "It's Tim."

A giddy tickle started in Liz's ribcage. She didn't look at her friends, but knew that Jazzy and Caitlin were watching her with amused expressions. In fact, was that a knowing grin Debbie was trying to hide behind her glass of Diet Coke?

Grandma drew herself up. "Tell him this is a girls-only party. No men allowed."

Liz rose. "I'll handle it."

She opened the door. When Tim caught sight of her, his eyes lit. Relief showed as he looked at her sweatshirt and jeans, and then lifted his glance to peer into the room behind her. "I'm glad you're not all in your pajamas."

Huh? "Why would we be in pj's?"

Tim looked confused. "I thought this was a pajama party."

Behind her, the room erupted with laughter. Hiding a grin, Liz explained, "Not pajamas. Lingerie. We're all giving Debbie gifts of lingerie. It's something girls do before a wedding."

Tim's face purpled. "Oh." He looked sideways, up, down, anywhere but at Liz. "I didn't know."

Liz couldn't help it. She giggled. "Did you need something, Tim?"

"Uh, yeah." He ducked his head and spoke to her in a low voice. "Could we talk out here? Privately?"

His worried expression chased Liz's giggles away. She sobered and followed him into the hallway.

When she had pulled the door closed, she leaned against it. A sudden fit of nerves threatened her composure, now that she was alone with him. All the emotions she'd wrenched up in front of Jazzy and Caitlin earlier were too raw, too fresh. She kept her gaze on the carpet between them.

"Turns out there's a connection between your pin and the man who was killed here two nights ago."

Liz's eyes snapped upward to fix on his face. "There is?"

He nodded. "Sheriff Daniels thinks Jason Sinclair was the one who broke into your apartment last December."

Liz's horror grew as Tim detailed the information the sheriff had uncovered.

When he finished, she shook her head, thoughts whirling. "I don't understand. Why would someone fly all the way across the country to steal a brooch hardly anyone knows about, which is only worth fifteen hundred dollars? I mean, our plane tickets out here cost almost four hundred dollars each and we got a bargain. If he rented a car on top of that, and stayed even one night in a hotel, he spent at least half the brooch's worth right there. It doesn't make sense."

Tim cocked his head. "Crime rarely makes sense. But I agree, there's got to be more to it than we know. Like, why didn't the guy try again, when he was unsuccessful in getting it the first time?"

Liz's mouth went uncomfortably dry as a thought crept into her mind. "Because somehow he knew I would be coming out here, where he lived. And he knew I'd have the brooch with me." She grabbed Tim's arm in a grip made strong by a sudden surge of fear. "How did he know, Tim? Has he been watching me all this time?"

She looked down the hallway, toward the corner. The hair on her arms rose. Was someone watching her even now? Not Jason Sinclair, but maybe the person who killed him? Or the one who had attacked her on the slopes?

Her throat seemed to squeeze shut as her suspicion became a certainty: the two were one and the same.

There was a killer after her.

A dry sob escaped her lips. In the next instant she was crushed to Tim's chest when he pulled her forward.

"Nothing is going to happen to you. I promise."

Though aware of Tim's warm arms encircling her, Liz couldn't suppress an icy shudder. "He tried to get me once. What if he's successful the next time?"

His hands gripped her forearms like steel vises. He pushed her back and ducked his head so she was forced to look up at him.

"First of all, the pin is locked away. You don't have it anymore." She opened her mouth to protest that the killer didn't know that, but he shushed her with a finger over her lips. "Second, there are two deputy sheriffs downstairs right now, watching every person who comes or goes in this lodge. And third, you're not going to be left alone for a minute. You're going to call me when you're ready to leave this party, and I'll escort you back to your room. And I'm sleeping on your sofa tonight."

A few hours ago Liz would have protested the need for anything so drastic as a bodyguard camped out in the condo. But after what she'd just heard, she wasn't about to refuse the offer.

She searched Tim's face. Her panic started to recede at the confidence she saw there. Tim always made her feel safe. "Thank you."

He nodded. "It's secure where it is tonight. Tomorrow morning you and I are going to take that pin to my bank and lock it in my safe-deposit box. And we'll let everybody know that you don't have it anymore. I'm sure Debbie and your grandmother will both agree that the bank is the safest place for it to stay until we catch the guy who's after it."

"That sounds like a good plan." The breath Liz drew shuddered, but she managed to hold back the tears that threatened to shatter her fragile grip on her nerves. "But let's don't tell them everything until after the wedding, okay? We'll just say that I had the brooch appraised, and after finding out how much it's worth, I felt it was safer in the bank until the wedding. I don't want Debbie to worry about anything."

"Agreed."

In the moment of silence that followed, Liz became acutely aware of Tim's hands on her arms. Heat from his palms seared through her sweatshirt and the skin beneath his grip tingled.

As though also aware of the contact, he released her and took a backward step. "So. You call me down in Ryan's room when you're ready to go to bed." His face flamed bright red. "Back to your condo, I mean."

Liz judged it safer not to speak. She nodded as she groped for the door handle behind her. Then she twisted it and slipped inside. Her hands trembled as she pulled the door shut behind her, but whether from fear or from being near Tim, she didn't know.

TWENTY-ONE

Liz let out a sigh of relief as she stepped up into Tim's vehicle, a green-and-white Ford Expedition with the Summit County Sheriff emblem on the side and a light bar mounted on the roof. She snapped her seat belt closed as Tim crossed to the driver's side. Large snowflakes fell in a thick white curtain all around them. Through the windshield, she caught a glimpse of the manager who'd just assisted them as he spoke with a teller inside the bank.

The driver's door opened and Tim climbed in. "There. That's a load off my mind."

She had to admit, she felt better having the brooch locked in Tim's safe-deposit box in the bank's vault. Even with a deputy sheriff on the couch in the other room, and her friends in the same room with her, she hadn't gotten much sleep. Though Jazzy insisted she must have, because she accused Liz of snoring half the night.

She'd stolen a curious look inside Tim's box when he'd opened it. In the back of her mind she had wondered if maybe he'd kept her engagement ring. If so, that would be the logical place to store it. But she'd only seen various papers, and a knife his grandfather had given him when he was a teenager. He'd probably sold the ring a long time ago.

"I agree. Now, let's just hope the killer finds out I don't have it anymore."

Tim turned the key and the engine sprang to life. Heat poured through the vent in the dashboard.

"We'll spread the word." He shifted into Reverse. "Though it's probably best we don't tell anyone exactly where it is. Except your grandmother and Debbie, of course."

"Grandma." Liz winced. "She is going to be really upset when I don't turn over official possession of the brooch to Debbie on Saturday."

"It can't be helped." Tim turned in his seat to look over his left shoulder as the vehicle backed up. "Besides, she wouldn't want to put either of her granddaughters in danger just for the sake of a piece of jewelry."

Tim had obviously forgotten what Grandma was like. "I don't know." Doubt colored Liz's words. "I mean, I know she wouldn't do anything that could hurt either of us. But she's really big on that family tradition."

Tim lifted a shoulder. "So you give unofficial possession to Debbie. Tell her as of Saturday the thing is hers, but it's being kept safe."

"I know!" Liz snapped her fingers. "Let's go pick up the appraisal. I can hand it over on Saturday. Debbie will need that anyway, to show her insurance company." She twisted her lips in a sour expression. "If I'd had the brooch appraised when I first got it, maybe I wouldn't be in this mess. I'd have kept it locked up somewhere."

Oops. Better not mention the circumstances surrounding her acquisition of the brooch. Liz turned her head toward the window so Tim couldn't see her face.

"You said the appraisal's being done by Alpine Jewelry over on Main?" Tim's voice was unruffled.

Relieved, Liz nodded. As they drove, she pointed through the window. "Look. We're starting to get some accumulation.

I hope it doesn't cause problems for Mom and Dad's plane." The cars in the parking lot they passed were blanketed with a couple of inches of snow.

"It won't. At least, not within the next few hours. We'll pick them up at one and get back up here before the roads can get bad."

And that would be interesting. Her parents loved Tim. When she showed up at the airport with him in tow, she would have some pretty pointed questions to answer.

The Expedition climbed up Main Street, which was practically deserted. Liz wondered at that, but then realized most vacationers would be out on the slopes today, enjoying the fresh snow. By tonight, the road would be bumper-to-bumper and the sidewalks shoulder-to-shoulder. Park City was always packed on Friday nights.

Tim parked directly in front of the jewelry store's door. He stomped on the parking brake and unsnapped his seat belt at the same time. "Sit tight," he told Liz as he got out.

She ignored him. He'd opened her door for her at the lodge, and again at the bank. This was starting to feel like a date. And it definitely was not. Though some traitorous notion in the back of her mind whispered, *It's awfully easy being with Tim again.* As he rounded the front of the vehicle, she opened her door and stepped down to the pavement.

A grin crept over his lips. "Stubborn woman."

She couldn't help returning the grin. *Yeah, awfully easy.*

When she headed for the store, he jumped ahead and swept open *that* door.

She surrendered with an easy laugh. "Fine. Be the gentleman, then." She didn't dare look at his face as she passed him.

The moment she stepped inside her nostrils tingled. She wrinkled her nose. What was that smell? Something like ammonia.

Mr. Cole stood waiting in the center of the showroom

when she entered. No sign of the sales clerk today. With one glance into his face, Liz became concerned. He looked awful. Red-rimmed eyes, pale skin. Was he sick?

"Mr. Cole, are you not feeling well?"

"What?" His eyes couldn't seem to settle on anything, but darted through the front window, and then to Tim and finally to her. "Oh. Yes, I'm fine. I got involved in a project last night and didn't get much sleep."

That explained the smell. Probably some chemical he used while he designed jewelry. Mr. Cole dug at his eyes with a thumb and forefinger, which succeeded in reddening them further. Then he peered at Tim.

Liz performed a quick introduction. "This is my friend, Tim Richards." As the two men shook hands, Liz continued, "Tim is a deputy sheriff here."

The corners of Mr. Cole's mouth lifted for a millisecond. "Yes, I thought as much. I saw you drive up in your police vehicle." The man pulled his hand back and shoved it into his pants pocket. He turned to Liz. "I was wrong about the value of your antique brooch."

"You were?" Liz's anticipation deflated a touch. "Is it not worth as much as you originally thought?"

"Oh, no. It's worth more. According to my research, the piece is definitely British, of the Georgian Era. I found a similar piece that sold in Europe recently for seventeen hundred. That's the value I've recorded on the appraisal document."

Liz shook her head. To think she'd been carrying seventeen hundred dollars around in her purse.

Mr. Cole straightened. "In light of that, I'd like to renew my offer from yesterday. I'll give you seventeen fifty for the brooch right now."

"I appreciate your offer, but no."

His nostrils flared. "All right. I'm prepared to go as high

as two thousand dollars. Cash." His eyes darted toward Tim. "That's unreported income, Miss Carmichael."

Liz hid a smile. "That's very generous of you, Mr. Cole, but the answer is no, regardless of the amount. The brooch isn't mine to sell."

Tim was staring at the man through eyes barely more than slits. "I'm curious. Why do you want it so badly?"

The man started. "Why, because it's a beautiful piece. The workmanship, the quality."

Liz offered an explanation. "Mr. Cole is a designer himself, so he appreciates quality."

"Hmm."

Tim nodded, but his expression told Liz he didn't buy that explanation. Liz wondered what made him so suspicious. Mr. Cole's offer convinced her even more that their theories were correct. If Mr. Cole, who was an expert, was so eager to purchase Grandma's brooch, it seemed more reasonable that someone else would want it badly enough to try to steal it.

But to kill a man and attack a woman for seventeen hundred dollars? No, Liz couldn't buy that. There was another explanation, one they hadn't uncovered yet.

"I understand," Mr. Cole told her. "If it were mine, I'd hold on to it, too." He paused, and a wistful expression stole over his face. "Do you mind if I look at it again? I'd love to examine those emeralds with my loupe."

"I'm sorry. I don't have it with me."

Mr. Cole's facial expression did not change, but a new stillness stole over him. "You don't?"

"No. After—"

"—after you told her the value yesterday, we decided carrying it around wasn't a good idea." Tim gave her a stern look. Apparently he didn't want her to mention the attack on the slopes yesterday.

"A wise decision, very wise." Mr. Cole cleared his throat.

"Let me get the appraisal certificate for you. I'll just be a moment." He took a backward step, watching Liz's face. "Ah, I hope you've put it someplace safe?"

Liz exchanged a tiny smile with Tim. Well, a *safe*-deposit box qualified, didn't it? "Don't worry. It's safe."

Duke watched through the front window as the deputy sheriff's vehicle pulled away from the curb. Only when it was out of sight did he allow his emotions to break free of the iron grip he held them in. He doubled over, his breath coming in gasps. Sweat beaded on his forehead and dampened his collar.

All that work last night for nothing. Not that his forgery, so quickly thrown together, would have fooled anyone who inspected it with more than a quick glance.

He straightened and sucked in air in deep draughts. His plan of substituting a forgery for the real Jersey Brooch had been a long shot. He knew that. If he had more time, he was confident he could duplicate the piece. But in eleven hours? It had been an impossible task at the outset.

Of course, now he had two days before he had to turn over the brooch. Did he dare…?

No. The man who'd made an international business of stealing valuable antique jewelry would recognize a fake in an instant.

He had failed. But there was still one last chance.

Duke whirled and almost ran into the back room. He dug the prepaid cell phone out of his jacket pocket and, with trembling fingers, punched in his associate's number.

The line was answered on the third ring. "Have you got it?"

His grip on the phone was so tight his hand trembled. Duke forced his fingers to relax. "No. And the situation has become serious. You promised you could—"

"Hey, wait just a minute. I promised she'd come, and she'd have the pin with her. That's all. I've done my part." The man's voice lowered. "And I want to know what happened to that guy I met on Wednesday. Did you do that?"

A hint of fear had crept into his associate's voice. Duke indulged in a cold smile. *Good. He shouldn't be the only one afraid.*

"Don't worry about him. Just worry about yourself—and the Carmichael girl. You've got to get that brooch."

"Me? No way. Not happening."

Duke lowered his voice and flooded it with as much menace as he could manage. "Listen to me. If I don't turn the Jersey Brooch over on Saturday, some very bad people are going to be very angry. And trust me, I'm not going down alone in this."

The breath that came through the phone sounded more like a choke. "All right. I'll see what I can do. I don't know how, but I'll—"

Duke disconnected the call. He didn't want to hear the man's plan. He didn't care. All he needed was the Jersey Brooch, and then he'd have no need for an associate anymore.

TWENTY-TWO

"Mom! Over here!"

Liz thrust her hand in the air and waved when she caught sight of her parents descending on the escalator in the Salt Lake International Airport. She rushed toward her parents when they stepped onto the floor. When she threw her arms around her mother, she was immediately enveloped in a sense of peace. These arms had loved and protected her through every turmoil life had thrown at her, from the moment she drew her first breath. The fear that had gripped her since the attack yesterday lifted. Which was stupid. What could her almost-fifty-year-old mother do to protect her against a vicious killer? Nothing, except probably put herself in danger, too.

Liz stiffened as the momentary peace faded. She had unconsciously prepared to spill her guts—and her heart—to Mom the moment they were together. But what would that accomplish? Nothing good. Both her parents would worry themselves sick if they thought she was in danger. They might even do something to endanger themselves in trying to shield her. The thought of that was intolerable. Better if they were kept unaware of the whole mess with the heirloom brooch until it was over.

Liz straightened from her mother's embrace and kissed her cheek, then moved on to her father.

"Honey, you look beautiful," Dad said as he swept her into a hug.

"Doesn't she?" Mom beamed at her for a moment, then deep lines creased her forehead. "What's wrong?"

Liz swallowed a groan. The sixth-sense mother thing in action. Mom always knew when something was up in Liz's life.

She pasted a relaxed grin on her face. "Not a thing. I've just been worried about you getting here safely. We're getting a lot of snow up in the mountains today."

"No problems at all," Dad said. "Smoothest flight I've ever had."

Mom studied her, suspicion apparent in her gaze. In the next moment, her forehead cleared and her eyes went round. "Oh my goodness, Ron, would you look who's here?"

Liz turned to see Tim emerge from the crowd behind them. In the next instant she was pushed aside as both her parents rushed past her. Dad grabbed Tim's hand while Mom threw her arms around him and hugged for all she was worth. A sense of outrage stole over Liz. Her parents had always adored Tim, but did they have to look so much happier to see him than they were to see her?

"You look great, son." Dad pumped Tim's hand like he was operating a car jack.

Mom finally pulled back from her embrace, still beaming. "We've been looking forward to seeing you at the wedding, but we had no idea you'd come with Liz to pick us up."

She turned a delighted grin on Liz, who focused on standing ramrod straight and keeping her face immobile. Mom had X-ray vision when it came to reading her only daughter. Liz knew if she let the slightest emotion show, Mom would be on her like a puppy on a chew toy.

"Actually," Tim began, "I had to bring Liz here today because—"

He was going to spill his guts. Liz jumped in.

"Because of the weather. Remember I mentioned the snow? Tim has four-wheel drive. In his police car. You knew he'd become a deputy sheriff, didn't you? In Summit County. That's up in Park City."

Why was she babbling? *Shut up, Liz. Mom's eyebrows are climbing.* She cast a silent plea toward Tim.

"Uh, that's right. The weather might get bad this afternoon." He pointed toward a baggage carousel behind them that had just started to move. "I think that's from your flight."

"Oh, good." Mom hooked her arm through Tim's and pulled him toward the carousel. "Tim, will you help Ron with my big bag? It's too heavy for him to lift, but he won't admit it. Can you believe the airline charged me a fee because they said it was over the limit? I think there was something wrong with their scales."

Dad put an arm around Liz's shoulders and followed. A tolerant smile twisted his lips as he watched his wife. "We're staying two nights, and she packed three bags. One of them's full of nothing but shoes."

Liz grinned and squeezed Dad's waist. Even if she couldn't confide everything, it sure was good to see her parents.

Tim let out an "Ummmph!" as he hefted the heavy suitcase into the back of the Expedition. "What does she have in that thing?"

Mr. Carmichael grinned and placed a smaller bag beside it. "I learned a long time ago it's best if we don't ask. You don't want to hear the explanation. It involves everything from the schedule of events to the weather, and hinges a great deal on what the other women are wearing. Husbands soon learn that wives think of their wardrobes as competition gear."

"I heard that, Ronald." From her position beside Liz in the backseat, Mrs. Carmichael turned to level a mock glare at her husband. "Keep it up and I'll feel the need to make a few wardrobe comments of my own, concerning that ridiculous green sweater you insisted on bringing but under no circumstances are allowed to wear in public."

"Yes, dear. Whatever you say."

Tim didn't bother to hide his smile as Mr. Carmichael tossed the last bag inside. The easy banter of these two reminded him of his own parents' thirty-five-year marriage. The first time he met the Carmichaels, he knew why he and Liz had immediately felt comfortable with each other. Their families were so similar.

He slammed the back doors and started to head around the driver's side of the vehicle. Mr. Carmichael stopped him with a hand on his shoulder. He glanced toward the women in the backseat and kept his voice low. "Mother called me yesterday and told me about the man who got shot up at the resort where we're staying. I didn't mention anything to Gail because I didn't want to upset her. But I have to admit, you being here with Liz today has me a little concerned." He peered into Tim's eyes. "Not that I'm not glad to see you two together, you understand."

Uh-oh. Better set that issue straight right now. "Sir, we're not really *together,* in any sense other than friends."

The man grinned. "Well, that's a start." Then he sobered. "So, between us, is everything okay at this resort?"

Tim scuffed his shoe against his vehicle's tire. "I hope so."

"You're not making me feel better, son." He shoved his hands in his pockets. "My family's not in any danger, are they?"

Tim looped his car keys over his index finger and jingled them. He knew Liz didn't want her parents to worry, but he couldn't be untruthful. "I promise you, I'll make sure nothing happens to her." Tim jerked his head upward, eyes going wide. "I mean to *them.*"

Mr. Carmichael's jaw tightened. "Tim, you and I are going to have a serious talk. Not right now, but later on tonight. And you're going to tell me everything. You hear?"

Tim hesitated. He didn't want to break any confidences with Liz, but the man had a right to know his daughter had been attacked and may be in danger. He intended to tell her so as soon as he could get her alone. Hopefully, before Mr. Carmichael cornered him and demanded some answers.

He nodded. "Yes, sir. I understand."

TWENTY-THREE

Liz slung her music portfolio over her shoulder and hefted her cello case. She lifted her chin and hollered toward the other room. "You girls about ready to go? We need to get downstairs to the reception hall and get tuned before the rehearsal starts."

She and Tim had arrived back at Eagle Summit Lodge ninety minutes ago from the airport with Mom and Dad, who were getting settled in Grandma's condo. Mom had tried to needle information out of her about Tim, but Liz was proud of herself for the way she'd handled it. She'd smiled and insisted they were just friends. The last thing she needed was to get her mother's hopes up about anything beyond a friendship between her and her handsome ex. Her mother's hopes—or her own. Anything else was just too painful to contemplate.

Caitlin came into the living room, her flute case in one hand and a collapsible music stand in the other. "I'm ready. Do you need help carrying anything?"

"No, thanks. I got it. Where's Jazzy?"

The petite violinist appeared at the mention of her name. "Right here."

"Okay, let's get going."

A knock sounded on the door when they reached it. Caitlin looked through the peephole before twisting the dead bolt open. "It's Debbie."

Liz's cousin pushed into the room. The skin around her eyes was tight, the corners of her mouth turned downward. "I need to talk to you. It's about that stupid heirloom thing." She crossed the living room and threw herself sideways across the chair.

Liz exchanged a glance with Caitlin and Jazzy. "You two go on and start getting set up. We'll be down in a minute."

As they left, she set her cello case down and let the leather portfolio slip off her shoulder to rest on the floor beside the couch.

The moment the door closed behind Liz's friends, Debbie launched into a loud lament. "Grandma is driving me absolutely insane! She's insisting I wear that hideous thing on my wedding dress tomorrow." She sat up and mimicked a high-pitched, nasal whine. *'I will not have my granddaughter break a six-generation family tradition.'* Aaahhh!" Debbie collapsed backward, her legs dangling over the arm of the chair. "Who cares about a stupid tradition anyway? This is *my* wedding, not hers!"

The proverbial prewedding jitters had finally overcome her sweet-natured cousin. Liz waited patiently for Debbie's rant to run itself out. When it did, she leaned forward to give the foot nearest her a comforting squeeze. "You don't have to wear the brooch on your dress. In fact, you can't."

That put a stop to the dramatic whimpering. Debbie sat upright and speared Liz with a hopeful gaze. "I can't?"

Liz shook her head. "I don't have it to give you."

Debbie's jaw dropped. "Don't tell me you lost the ugly thing. Girl, she's going to kill you."

"No, I didn't lose it." Liz paused. No sense upsetting an already anxious bride. "But yesterday I paid a visit to Mr. Cole and had it appraised. I figured you'd need an official appraisal for your insurance policy or something." Not necessarily untrue, but a gross understatement of the real reason for the appraisal.

"Really? How much is it worth?"

"You're not going to believe this. Seventeen hundred dollars."

Debbie's mouth gaped open. "No way."

Liz nodded. "After I found out how much the brooch is worth, I didn't feel comfortable carrying it around. Tim and I locked it in his safe-deposit box at the bank." Liz couldn't believe she was about to make this offer, but if this is what it took to keep her cousin out of the danger the possession of that brooch included… "You tell Grandma you'll wear the brooch. That'll get her off your back. Then I'll conveniently forget to pick it up at the bank. The wedding isn't until four o'clock tomorrow. By then the bank will be closed until Monday morning."

Tears glittered in Debbie's eyes. "You'd do that for me? Bear the brunt of Grandma's anger? She'll never forgive you, Liz."

But Liz knew she would. One day, when the police had caught the murderer and had him safely behind bars, the truth could come out. Then maybe she'd be restored to Grandma's good graces.

For now, she lifted a shoulder. "She's never forgiven me for breaking the tradition the last time. I can handle it."

Debbie flew across the space between them and caught Liz in a breath-stopping hug. "You are so awesome. How can I thank you?"

Liz returned the embrace, then pushed her gently back. "You can calm down and enjoy your wedding."

Last night's happiness returned to Debbie's eyes. "You've got a deal. Let's get down to the rehearsal."

Liz grabbed her cello and followed Debbie out the door. She stopped long enough to lock the dead bolt before they headed down the hallway for the elevator. When the door slid open, Debbie stepped inside.

Liz halted. "I forgot my music. I'm just going to run get it. You go ahead."

"Here, let me take your cello."

Liz handed Debbie the instrument case and jogged back down the hallway to her condo. She let herself in. Yep, there was her portfolio, beside the couch. Right where she'd left it. She scooped it up, slung the strap over her shoulder and whirled around. She jerked the door open and almost ran through the doorway…and knocked right into someone standing in the hallway.

Fear jolted through her insides.

Then she looked up. Her muscles relaxed, and she heaved an exaggerated sigh. "Jeremy, you just about scared the life out of me."

He flashed the smile she remembered so well, the one that exuded Irish charm. "Sorry, Lizzie. Oops." He held up a finger. "I mean, Liz."

Liz hefted the strap on her shoulder. "What are you doing here? Are you going to the wedding rehearsal?" Things could get pretty uncomfortable with both Tim and Jeremy in the same room all evening.

His forehead creased. "Rehearsal? No. I need to talk to you."

That was a relief. "Okay, but it'll have to wait. I need to get downstairs. The rehearsal is going to start in a few minutes."

"No, you don't understand." His eyes flickered sideways. "This can't wait."

Liz opened her mouth to protest, but in the next moment Jeremy grabbed her arm in a strong grip. His other hand twisted the doorknob behind her. The door opened, and Liz found herself shoved backward into the condo.

"What do you think you're doing?" Liz jerked her arm out of his grasp.

"I'm sorry, Liz, really. But I need your help in the worst way."

She rubbed the skin on her arm where he'd gripped her. He sounded really desperate. In fact, he looked desperate as he stood leaning against the door, staring at her. She'd never seen happy-go-lucky Jeremy wear such a panicky, pinched expression.

She swept a hand to indicate the door behind him. "Well, this is not a good way to ask for my help. Now let me get down to the rehearsal and I'll meet you someplace later, when it's over." She tilted her head to give him a stern look. "In a public place."

His jaw moved as he chewed on the inside of his lip. Then he shook his head. "This can't wait. I know this is going to sound like a strange question, but do you still have that old antique pin your grandmother gave you?"

The room seemed to tilt as blood drained out of Liz's brain.

"Pin?" Liz's voice came out in a squeak.

"Come on, Liz. Don't play games. Do you still have it, or have you already given it to Debbie?"

Liz's fingers curled into fists. No way was she going to get Debbie involved in this mess. She'd forgotten that Jeremy knew about the pin. She'd told him three years ago, showed it to him, even. In fact, she'd cried on his shoulder over the whole messy episode, when Grandma was being so nasty about her disregard for her family's tradition, when she broke her engagement with Tim.

Was Jeremy somehow involved in the attempts to steal her brooch? If so, that meant he was involved in the attack on her yesterday, and…she gulped. And in the murder of Jason Sinclair.

She forced herself to respond calmly. "No. I haven't turned it over to Debbie."

"That's a relief." His cheeks puffed with a gust of breath. His glance circled the condo. "So where is it?"

"It isn't here. I put it in a safe place."

A dangerous glint flashed in his green eyes. "Don't mess around, Liz. You don't know what you're dealing with."

Though her insides quaked, Liz steeled her voice. "I think I have an idea."

His shoulders heaved in a silent laugh. "No, you really don't. Listen, just give me the pin and this will all blow over. You can tell your family you went to get it and somebody had stolen it. I'll even split the money with you. Twenty-five thousand dollars. As soon as I get it, I swear I'll give you half."

Liz blinked. *Twenty-five thousand dollars?* For a seventeen-hundred-dollar brooch?

"Jeremy, even if I wanted to give it to you, I couldn't. I don't have it. Tim and I locked it in a bank vault this morning."

He went still. A bead of sweat glistened as it slid down his red face. "Oh, Liz. I hope you're kidding. 'Cause if not, I don't know what they're going to do to me. Or you, either."

She shook her head. None of this made sense. Including Jeremy's involvement. He'd never been violent. Sometimes a jerk, but not violent. Not unless he'd changed a bunch in three years.

She watched him carefully as she asked, "Was it you who attacked me on the slopes?"

He swiped his sleeve across his damp forehead. "What are you talking about? Someone attacked you?"

"Yesterday. A man followed me to an isolated place, knocked me to the ground and tried to take my backpack." She watched him carefully. "The police think it was the same person who murdered that man Wednesday night."

He started visibly. "That wasn't me. Honest. I had nothing to do with that."

The renewed vigor with which he chewed the inside of his lip convinced Liz that he was telling the truth. A tiny thread of relief worked its way into her tense muscles. Jeremy was somehow involved, but he hadn't actually hurt anybody. Yet.

The desperation she saw in his wild eyes left her no confidence that he wouldn't harm someone in the future. Starting, maybe, with her.

Options! Options! What are my options?

Scream. But that would do no good at all. Since most everyone had checked out of the lodge after the discovery of the body, this hallway was deserted except for the wedding party. And they were all downstairs at the rehearsal. No matter how loudly she screamed, nobody would hear her.

Could she run? He stood between her and the door. No way she could get around him and out into the hallway.

A frantic prayer formed in her mind. *Lord, please help me. I've got to get out of here.*

What about making a run for it in here? If she dashed for the bedroom, she might make it. She could slam the door, lock it and call 9-1-1. The deputy sheriffs downstairs could be up here in a matter of minutes. Liz glanced toward the bedroom, her mind busy planning her path. She had a clear shot between the couch and the dinette table. He'd be after her the second she moved. She could count on a three-step lead at the most, and her knee was still bothering her from yesterday. Still, it was the best shot she had.

She tensed her muscles and sprinted.

Before she completed her first step, Jeremy was moving. She hadn't gone two yards when he overtook her. He got a grip on the music portfolio still hanging from her shoulder and used it to jerk her backward. She was flung sideways, over the back of the couch. In the next instant, Liz's face was pressed into the fabric cushion. Rage and terror gathered in her chest and exploded out of her in a scream. But Jeremy's strong hand pressed her head down, and the sound was muffled by the cushion. His weight crushing her, he jerked her left arm up behind her. Her scream changed to a cry of pain as the movement wrenched her shoulder muscles into an unnatural position.

Jeremy's voice sounded close to her ear. "I really don't want to hurt you, Liz. But you're not leaving me a choice."

TWENTY-FOUR

Tim came into the reception hall on the heels of Debbie's father, freshly showered and changed from his quick visit home after dropping the Carmichaels off, and seeing Liz safely to her grandmother's condo. He arched his back, stretching tense muscles. A night on a lumpy couch and a lot of tension had created more than a few knots. He needed to get to the gym to work the stress out of his body.

Most of the group had already assembled. The bride and groom stood to one side of the room, Ryan nodding his head while Debbie pointed toward the rows of chairs. Liz's father and uncle were enjoying a family reunion, clapping each other's shoulders and exclaiming over their thinning hair, while their mother watched her sons with a proud smile. Ryan's family watched the reunion from the far corner. The bridesmaids stood talking to a man who held a big black bible—the pastor, obviously—while the groomsmen had each collapsed over a row of chairs. Tim grinned. They'd apparently had a pretty late night, playing games after he left to camp out on Liz's couch.

At the far end of the room, Liz's friends sat behind metal music stands tuning their instruments. A third chair, the one on the right, was empty.

A frantic jolt kicked Tim's pulse up a notch. He scanned the room again.

Liz was not here.

He marched over to her mother.

"There you are, Tim." She smiled up at him. "I hope we have time to catch up later. Maybe we can sit beside each other at dinner?"

"Yes, ma'am." Tim gave her a distracted smile. "Um, where's Liz?"

Her head turned in a smooth arc as she looked around the room. "Why, she's not here, is she? I'm sure she'll be—"

Tim didn't wait to hear what Mrs. Carmichael was sure of. He hurried up the center aisle toward Liz's friends.

"Where is she?" he asked with a glance at her empty chair.

Caitlin adjusted the music on her stand. "We left her up in the condo talking to Debbie. They'll be along in a minute."

"Debbie's over there."

Two heads jerked up as Jazzy and Caitlin looked where Tim pointed. The sudden widening of their eyes told him all he needed to know. He whirled and almost ran across the room to Liz's cousin.

Steady. Don't alarm them. Liz wouldn't like that.

He forced what he hoped was a calm smile. "Hey, Deb. Have you seen Liz?"

Debbie turned a distracted glance toward him. "Liz? Yes, she's over—oh. That's funny. She was right behind me. I carried her cello down and she went back to get her music." She pointed toward the corner, where a cello case leaned against a wall.

Tim fought a surge of alarm. "She went back to her room?"

"Yeah. And I stopped by the front desk to ask Mr. Harrison a couple of things about the setup on my way back." Debbie's brow wrinkled. "But that was at least fifteen minutes ago. I wonder what's keeping her."

Ryan lifted a shoulder. "Maybe she—"

Tim didn't wait to hear his theory. He dashed out of the room, not caring that everyone's eyes were fixed on him as he left.

Liz's foot nearly missed the next step. She stumbled, and gasped at the pain that shot through her shoulder—as much as she could gasp past her gag. Jeremy had grabbed the nearest thing he could, a cloth napkin from the dinette table, and had shoved the whole thing in her mouth. Then he'd jerked her to her feet and forced her through the door, her arm twisted painfully behind her.

Tears of rage blurred her vision. How dare he treat her like this? They had been sweethearts once. Her foot nearly missed another step.

"Watch where you're going," he hissed in her ear. "And hurry up. I don't want to run into anybody in this stairwell."

He forced her down four flights of stairs in a stairwell at the rear of the building, but instead of exiting on the ground floor, he kept going. Liz didn't even know this building had a basement.

As though he read her mind, Jeremy's voice sounded from close behind her head. "Kate brought me down here a couple of times on her break. She's not nearly as big a prude as you were, Lizzie."

Eeewww. Best not think about that. Focus instead on keeping her shoulder muscles tight so he didn't jerk her arm out of its socket.

At the bottom of the stairs, Jeremy reached around her and pulled open a heavy fire door. In the next moment he pushed her through, his hold on her arm still unbreakable. The door closed behind them, plunging Liz into darkness.

Tim didn't bother with the elevator. He poured on the speed and ran down the short hallway from the reception room to the lobby. Then he banged through the fire door into the stairwell, and took the stairs two at a time all the way up to the fourth floor. Before he reached the top he heard a door close behind him, and the clatter of feet echoing on the steps. As he rounded a floor he saw Liz's friends below him hurrying to catch up.

His breath came in painful gasps by the time he reached the top, whether from the exertion or fear for Liz, he didn't know. He didn't let breathlessness stop him, but burst into the fourth-floor hallway and dashed toward the door to Liz's condo.

It was unlocked.

The lump in his stomach took on the weight of lead. She wouldn't leave herself exposed with an unlocked door, not after being attacked on the slopes yesterday.

He ran inside, his gaze sweeping the empty room.

"Liz! Are you in here?"

A hollow silence answered. Heart thudding behind his ribcage, Tim dashed through the place. He checked both bedrooms, both bathrooms, even the closets. All empty.

He returned to the main room in time to see Jazzy and Caitlin run through the doorway. And the person on their heels made Tim look away with a cringe.

How could he face Liz's father, when less than two hours ago he'd promised to take care of her?

TWENTY-FIVE

A dim light flipped on. Liz got a brief glimpse of concrete floors and rows of housekeeping carts before she was shoved into a smaller room. Discarded furniture filled most of the floor space. A stack of old mattresses lined the back corner.

"Here. Sit down."

Jeremy pulled a scratched dinette chair into the clear space in the center of the floor and pushed her down into it. Fresh pain shot through her shoulder at the sudden release. Her cry was muffled by the napkin wadded in her mouth.

Jeremy ran his hand through his hair, panic whitening the skin between his eyes as he stared down at her. "Honest, Liz, I didn't mean for this to happen. But I don't know what else to do. I've got to get that pin. You have no idea what I'm up against."

If he hoped to make her feel sorry for him, he could forget it. Liz was too frightened and angry to be moved by pity. Especially toward the man who'd gagged her and tried to rip her arm out of its socket. Besides, she'd already told him she couldn't give him Grandma's brooch. She reached up to pull the gag out of her mouth to tell him so again.

Jeremy saw her. He put one hand on the back of her head and pushed it back in with the other. "Sorry, but I can't risk you screaming. Sound echoes down here, and I saw a couple of cop cars out front when I arrived. Good thing I had the fore-sight to make a copy of Kate's keys, otherwise I wouldn't have had the nerve to come up to your room."

He looked around and then went to a pile of laundry in the corner. The towel he picked up was frayed. He pulled out a pocket knife and sawed through one edge, then ripped it lengthwise.

"This ought to keep you quiet," he said as he folded one of the strips and covered her mouth, gag and all. Tears stung Liz's eyes when he pulled it tight around her head and tangled her hair in the knot. The wadded napkin filled her entire mouth, and she gagged as it pressed against the back of her throat. Her tongue felt cottony, every bit of moisture absorbed by the fabric.

Fear mounted as she watched him pace with quick, frantic steps. This was not the Jeremy she knew. That guy would not have hurt anyone. This one looked desperate, like he was ready to fall to pieces. Like he was capable of anything.

His pacing stopped suddenly. He seemed to come to a decision. Feet planted in front of her, he pulled a slim cell phone out of the back pocket of his jeans.

"I have no choice," he told her as he punched buttons. "I don't know what else to do. This was not supposed to be my job. I did the research, got the proof. That was supposed to be the end of it."

Research? What did that mean? Jeremy was employed as a researcher, but last she heard from Debbie, he still held the same job he'd landed right after they graduated from college. He did statistical research related to economics and housing trends, boring stuff like that. Certainly nothing remotely con-nected to jewelry.

He held the phone to his ear. "Yeah, I got her." Pause. "No, not the pin. Her. She doesn't have it."

He jerked the phone away from his ear with a grimace. Liz

heard a male voice shouting on the other end, though she couldn't make out the words.

"She says she locked it in a bank vault or something. Listen, you're going to have to come deal with this. I've done everything I can."

Liz's heart sank to her toes as she listened to Jeremy give directions for slipping into the basement of the lodge without passing the deputy sheriffs upstairs.

Tim, where are you? I need help!

"Tim, you have thirty seconds to tell me what's going on. Where is my daughter?"

Mr. Carmichael's stern expression warned Tim that the man would not accept vague explanations. Time to come clean.

"I don't know where she is, sir. I'll tell you everything. But I have to call the sheriff first."

The man paled. "Why do you have to call the sheriff?"

Tim didn't waste any more precious seconds, but pulled out his phone and dialed his boss's number. Caitlin and Jazzy each placed comforting hands on Liz's father's arms, their anxiety apparent in the gazes they fixed on Tim.

"Daniels."

Tim wasted no time with greetings. "She's missing. We need a team out here to search this place top to bottom. Dogs, too."

"Slow down, Richards. Feed me the facts one at a time."

Sheriff Daniels's even tone acted like a cool cloth on Tim's burning mind. He walked into the kitchen area, mostly so he could turn his back on the alarm blossoming on Mr. Carmichael's face.

He forced himself to speak slowly. "Miss Carmichael was last seen fifteen minutes ago in her rented condo at Eagle Summit Lodge. She failed to appear for the wedding rehearsal. The last person to see her was her cousin, who said she returned to the condo to get her music."

Tim twisted around and scanned the room. He spotted a black leather folder with a shoulder strap on the floor beside the couch. He turned toward Liz's friends with an unspoken question, and Caitlin nodded.

"That's her portfolio."

Tim swallowed, then told the sheriff, "The music she was after is still here."

"Anything missing? Look out of place?"

He relayed the question to the others.

"A napkin," Jazzy said instantly. "From the table. There were four."

Sure enough, pale green folded cloth napkins sat before three of the four chairs. The fourth was missing.

Both girls disappeared into the back bedrooms while Tim told the sheriff about the napkin.

"Did she have the jewelry on her?" the sheriff asked.

"No, sir. We locked it in my safe-deposit box this morning."

Caitlin and Jazzy returned to the living area. "Looks like everything else is here," Jazzy said.

"Her jacket is still hanging in the closet," Caitlin added.

Mr. Carmichael put his hands together and covered his mouth with his fingertips, as though in prayer. But his eyes never left Tim.

"Nothing else is missing," Tim told his boss. "Only Liz."

"All right. I'm sending in a team. Secure that room and meet me in the lobby in fifteen minutes. I'll call the two men on-site there and have them shut the place down. Nobody in or out."

Tim glanced at his watch. Ten past four. The slopes had just closed, which meant skiers would be coming down off the mountain right about now. If there were any who were staying at the lodge, they wouldn't be happy about not being able to get to their rooms.

Tough. Liz's life might be at stake.

"Yes, sir. I'll see you in fifteen."

He disconnected the call and announced to the three people watching him, "Okay, everybody out of here. We've got to secure this room."

"Now, wait just a minute." Mr. Carmichael's jaw had the same stubborn set Tim had seen so often in his daughter. "Nobody's going anywhere until you tell me what's going on."

Alarm pulsed along Tim's nerves. He didn't have time for explanations. Everything in him whispered that every minute counted, that they had to find Liz quickly. But her father deserved to know the danger.

"Come on." He jerked his head toward the door as he started to move. "I'll explain on the way downstairs."

TWENTY-SIX

Jeremy shredded a couple more towels into strips with his pocket knife and knotted them together. As he used them to tie Liz's hands behind her, she tried to control the panic rising like acid into her throat. She couldn't make herself believe, even now, that Jeremy would really hurt her. Especially not for a piece of jewelry. Surely he placed some value on their former relationship.

But she knew nothing about whomever he had called.

When her hands had been secured behind her back, Jeremy stood in front of her. "Liz, I never meant for things to go this far."

Unable to speak, she glared up at him.

"Honest. It all started a year or so ago when I met this guy on a chairlift over at Park City Mountain Resort. We got to talking on the ride up, and he told me he was a jeweler. He was telling me all about making jewelry and picking out good diamonds and how a well-made piece of jewelry is like art or something, worth way more than just the value of the gold and stones it's made of."

A jewelry maker? Liz straightened in the hard chair. A memory surfaced, an image of Mr. Cole's wide eyes as he examined Grandma's brooch.

"I don't know anything about that stuff. The only jewelry

I ever saw that was interesting was that pin your grandmother gave you. So I told him about it. It was just something to talk about to kill time on a long lift ride, you know?"

Liz could almost hear the conversation. Jeremy always had wanted people to think he knew more than he did.

"So he starts asking me questions, like how old it was and all that, and he tells me if that pin's origin could be proved, it might be worth a lot of money." Jeremy pulled another chair from the stack of dilapidated furniture. He straddled it, facing her. "Well, you know that's what I do, Liz. I'm a researcher. True, I didn't know anything about jewelry, but I know how to research. And I have a lot of free time on my hands, working for the government. So a couple of days later I decided to research your pin. I went down to the Family History Library and traced your family tree. And you know what? I traced your genealogy all the way back to England in the late 1700s."

In spite of the gag and the raw places the rough strips of terry cloth were rubbing on her wrists, a spark of interest kept Liz focused on his story. She could picture Jeremy doing all the things he described. Going to the Family History Library in downtown Salt Lake, where the LDS Church, otherwise known as the Mormons, maintained the world's largest collection of genealogical records. Spending hours on the Internet. It was the kind of stuff he'd always liked to do.

"And you're not going to believe what I found out, Liz." A smirk twisted his lips. "You've got some pretty notorious ancestors. Have you ever heard of King George IV of England?"

Well, duh. Everybody knew about the kings of England. Liz nodded.

"Ever heard of his famous mistress, Lady Jersey?"

Liz shook her head. Where was this going?

"At first I thought you might be related to British royalty."

Jeremy snickered. "But it turns out you're just related to the mistress. Lady Jersey was pretty notorious back in the late 1700s, and she had a lot of influence over old Georgie when he first married. When George commissioned a jeweled pin as a wedding gift for his new wife, Caroline of Brunswick, Lady Jersey threw a fit. So George commissioned an identical one for her." He leaned forward over the chair back. "I actually located a satire sketch from that time period showing both Lady Jersey and Caroline of Brunswick wearing the matching pins. Do you know what that means?"

Liz could guess. This pin was worth a lot more than the value Mr. Cole quoted her. If it could be proved that her family's brooch was one of the two, and if someone managed to gain possession of both pieces *and* the proof…

"Those two pins together, along with the sketch, are worth well over half a million dollars." Jeremy rested his chin on his hands on top of the chair. "What do you think about that?"

I think you're a jerk and an idiot. She let her disgust show in her eyes.

Jeremy snorted and shook his head. "I figured you'd at least be impressed with my research. Anyway, after a few years, George got himself another girlfriend and sent Lady Jersey packing. She kept the pin, of course, and when her daughter got married, she gave it to her as a wedding gift. That's how your family tradition got started. Lady Jersey's daughter was your great-great-great-great-great-grandmother."

A buzz sounded loud in the concrete room. Jeremy jerked to his feet. Tendons in his neck corded visibly when he read the text on the screen of his cell phone.

"Come on." His voice was tight. "He's here. We've got to meet him outside."

The fear that had receded during Jeremy's story returned and sent a wave of nausea through Liz's stomach. She sucked in a deep breath through her nose and fought the urge to vomit. If she threw up with this gag in her mouth, she'd choke to death. Liz's legs wobbled unsteadily as he pulled her to her feet.

Jeremy marched her out of the little room into the long, cluttered hotel basement. He led her to the far end, toward a large metal exit. From its position, Liz knew it would let them outside on the corner nearest the slopes. She tried to picture that side of the building. It was opposite the lobby, as far away from the front entrance as they could get. Beyond that corner of the building was the tree-lined trail where…she gulped. Where she had seen a man cross the snow toward Jason Sinclair's body two days ago. This corner of the building was secluded. Bare.

A sob escaped her throat, but went unheard because of the gag.

The heavy door to the stairwell they'd come down was just a few yards away, alongside a service elevator. If she wrenched away from Jeremy's grip, could she get to it?

No. Her hands were secured behind her back. Even if she could gain the door before he stopped her, she'd never get it open.

They approached the exit. Jeremy leaned in front of her and pulled it open by the handle. An icy blast of air hit Liz in the face and sent a shiver through her frame. Jeremy leaned through the door to look outside.

Behind them, the other door opened. Liz jerked around. When she caught sight of the person who stepped through, her knees went weak.

TWENTY-SEVEN

Tim stood in the lobby surrounded by Liz's family, his hands clenched into fists. Four deputies clustered together by the front entrance, pelting Mr. Harrison with questions. Tim half-listened, his gaze glued to the door. Where was the sheriff?

Liz's grandmother stepped in front of him, her handbag dangling from her arm. She glowered up at him from beneath formidable gray eyebrows. "Young man, I insist you tell me what this is all about this instant. Where is my granddaughter?"

Tim tried to get a grip on his panic. His instructors at the academy had taught him the importance of maintaining a sense of calm in the face of anxious loved ones.

But they didn't tell me what to do if the missing person was someone I loved.

Tim set his teeth together. "I wish I knew, Mrs. Carmichael."

The front entrance opened, and Tim's gaze flew in that direction. But it was just another deputy. This was taking way too long.

Debbie's father took Mrs. Carmichael's hand. "Mother, I want you to come over here and sit down. Ron is going to fill us in. Let Tim go talk to the other police officers and see if he can help."

Tim threw him a grateful glance as he hurried away. He couldn't help looking toward the fireplace, where Liz's dad stood with his arm around his wife. The agony in both of their faces forced him to look away.

Tim jogged across the lobby to join the deputies. "What's the holdup?" He didn't bother to filter the anger out of his voice. "Daniels should have been here by now."

"He just radioed," Farmer told him. "He got delayed by the traffic and the weather. But he's minutes away."

Tim's hands fisted and unfisted with pent-up energy. "This is taking too long. We should have started searching the building by now."

Adam Goins clapped a hand on his arm. "Calm down, Richards. He'll be here in two minutes."

Tim ground his teeth. Easy for them to say. Liz could be in one of the condos in this building right now, suffering who-knew-what at the hands of a murderer.

He whirled and marched away, aware that they all stared after him. Near the front desk, Mr. Harrison hovered. If a man could look more miserable than Liz's family, the resort owner managed to do it. He wrung his hands as Tim came toward him.

"I can't believe this is happening." He shook his head. "What can I do? How can I help find Miss Carmichael before…"

Tim swallowed. No need to finish the thought. He massaged his temples with a thumb and a forefinger. The sheriff would arrive any minute and start spouting orders. They'd search the building starting on the ground floor, this floor. What would they need?

"A passkey," he barked. "The sheriff is going to need a passkey to get into every room."

The creases in Mr. Harrison's brow deepened. "Even the ones with guests? Without a warrant I don't know—" Tim's glare cut him off. He gulped. "I'll get it."

He turned to head back behind the front desk, and Tim followed.

"He'll want to start on this floor, if that makes a difference. He'll work from the bottom up."

Mr. Harrison extracted a ring of keys from his pocket and grasped one between his fingers. He spoke as he fitted it into the lock of a drawer. "Then they won't start on this floor. There's a basement. Directly below us are the furnace and hot water heaters, and the back end is used mostly for equipment and storage."

Tim's mind grasped the information. Normally he wouldn't dare make a move without orders from his superiors. But this wasn't a normal situation. This was *Liz*. He could get down there and check out the basement, get a head start on the search. It beat standing around here waiting, where each second of inactivity seemed to stretch into an hour.

"How do you get to the basement?"

Mr. Harrison pointed toward the far hallway. "There's a service elevator at the back end of the building that house-keeping uses."

Tim nodded toward the key in the drawer the man had just opened. "When the sheriff gets here, give him that and tell him where I went."

He jogged in the direction the resort owner had pointed. Around the corner. Past the elevators. Around another corner. Down a long corridor, past a dozen or so doors to the lodge's first-floor condominiums. When he rounded another corner he caught sight of the service elevator at the end of that hallway. He hadn't even realized this was back here. Or the stairwell beside it. He threw open the door and ran down the stairs. The echo of his steps sounded loud in his ears.

He leaped off the bottom step and toward the fire door. With his hand on the handle, he paused as his training kicked in. He was wearing his service weapon, as he always did. But he wasn't wearing a vest. He never did off duty. He could run back upstairs for one, but that would waste precious minutes. No way he'd let lack of a vest stop him from looking for Liz, but he should use caution.

He unholstered his weapon and held it in his right hand while he gripped the lever-style steel handle and pushed it down slowly with his left. The click as the fastener disengaged sounded loud in the stairwell. He forced himself to wait a couple of seconds before pulling the door toward him in excruciatingly slow motion. An inch. That's all. Just enough to see through. He put his eye to the crack. A moment to focus in the dim light.

What he saw on the other side made him forget caution. He jerked the door open and charged through.

"Tim!"

Liz's scream rang inside her head, but the gag kept any sound from escaping. She twisted away from Jeremy, but couldn't dislodge his grip on her arm. Her captor's hold tightened, horror spreading across his features as though his doom was charging toward him holding a gun. Which, Liz decided with no small amount of satisfaction, it was.

Tim was still six feet away, advancing on them with his gun pointed at Jeremy, when a voice spoke close behind Liz's ear. "That's far enough, I think."

Tim stopped midstep, his gaze fixed on a point just behind Liz. He lowered his foot toward the floor immediately.

Jeremy's hold on Liz tightened at the same moment cold steel pressed against the side of her neck. She didn't need to turn around to know who was standing behind her. She recognized the voice. Mr. Cole.

And he held a gun to her head.

TWENTY-EIGHT

Jeremy released his grip on Liz's arm and stepped away, his eyes round as basketballs. She didn't dare move. Though Mr. Cole didn't touch her, his gun held her captive more expertly than Jeremy's fist.

"Deputy, I'll ask you to lay your gun carefully on the floor." Mr. Cole's voice held a deadly calm. Tim hesitated only a moment before he complied.

"Thank you. Norville, you certainly have made a mess of things. Even Sinclair could have handled the situation better than this."

Jeremy licked his lips, his gaze fixed on the weapon at Liz's throat. "I told you. I'm not a crook. I'm a researcher."

Mr. Cole's chuckle rumbled behind Liz. "The two are hardly mutually exclusive. Especially in this instance."

Tim looked ready to explode. "Cole, let her go."

So he'd recognized the jewelry store owner, too.

"Much as I'd like to do that, deputy, I just don't see how I can."

Tim splayed his fingers and held his hands up. "If you let Liz go, we'll give you a head start before we sound the alarm. You have my word."

"I appreciate the offer, but I'm afraid I have to decline."

"Look, this place is swarming with cops." Out of the corner of her eye Liz saw Jeremy jump. She kept her eyes fixed on Tim. "In a few minutes they're going to start a room-by-room search. And they're going to begin with this floor. You can't escape. If you let Liz go, I'll delay them. Buy you enough time for a decent head start."

Mr. Cole's hand came up beneath Liz's arm. The gun barrel pressed closer to her skin, which set her heart thumping.

"Thank you for the reminder. We've got to get out of here. Norville, is that your Jeep just outside the door here?" Jeremy's gulp was loud as he nodded. "Good. You drive. Deputy, you take the passenger side." He leaned close enough to press his chest against Liz's shoulder blades. When he spoke, his breath warmed the back of her ear. "Miss Carmichael and I are going to get cozy in the backseat."

Liz was tugged backward through the door. A heavy snow fell and clung to her bare head and shoulders in the short walk from the door to a Jeep Cherokee parked a few feet away. No other cars were in sight. This entrance was nothing more than a loading dock, and was completely deserted. A flashing red light to her left drew her attention. Hope swelled for a moment, but then she realized it was a reflection. The front of the lodge lay around the corner and all the way at the other side of the building. She shivered as the wind shifted and blew large flakes into her face, momentarily blinding her.

Mr. Cole pulled her to a stop beside the car. "Before we get in, deputy, I'd like you to empty your pockets. Give everything to your friend, here. Cell phone, pocket knife, wallet. And weapons, of course."

Tim's chin jerked upward defiantly.

Mr. Cole went on. "If you're considering an act of heroism, I wouldn't advise it. You see, I don't have anything to lose at this point. A very nasty man is coming to pick up the Jersey Brooch in less than forty-eight hours. I fear him far more than I do the justice system."

The Jersey Brooch. That stupid family heirloom was the cause of all this trouble. If Liz ever saw the thing again, she'd grind it beneath her heel.

Without a word, Tim did as Mr. Cole directed. Jeremy took the items Tim shoved at him and then unlocked the Jeep with a remote. Liz noticed the fearful glances he kept throwing toward Mr. Cole, the quick obedience he exhibited as he followed every direction. He refused to meet her gaze when he opened first the rear door and then the driver's.

On Mr. Cole's instruction, Liz climbed into the backseat at the same moment Tim sat in the front passenger seat. Her arm was not freed for even a fraction of a second, though the gun did slide from her neck to her temple as her captor slid in beside her. No comfort there.

As Jeremy backed out of the loading dock, Mr. Cole directed, "Take the back trail, Norville, the one that runs around the south side of the resort. You know it?"

He nodded. "I don't know if we can get through with this snow, though."

"Put it in four-wheel. We'll get through. Unless you're as incompetent at driving as you are at retrieving jewelry."

From her position in the center of the back seat, Liz saw Jeremy's hands tighten on the steering wheel. But he pressed the 4x4 button on the dash and steered the car toward a narrow access trail in the opposite direction from the front of the lodge. Panic threatened to choke Liz when she glanced over her shoulder and saw the flashing red lights—and her hopes—fade.

A series of sniffles came from the backseat. Tim's heart wrenched when he realized Liz was crying.

"At least untie her and take the gag off." He put a note of pleading into his voice.

"How thoughtless of me. No sense being barbaric about this."

As the vehicle plowed through a shallow snowdrift at the end of the access road, Tim twisted in his seat to hold Liz's gaze with his, as Cole worked with one hand to untie the knot at the back of her head. Even in the fading light Tim saw the terror in her swollen pupils. He forced a smile.

Lord, don't let her get hurt. Help us out of this mess.

When Cole unwound the white strip, Liz worked her mouth to spit out the wad of fabric. Cole reached up with his free hand and pulled it. Pale green. The missing napkin. Tim sent a vicious glare in Jeremy's direction at the reminder of Liz's abduction. Rage overtook his thoughts as Liz gulped noisy draughts of air. His short fingernails dug into the fleshy part of his palms. If he ever got Jeremy alone he'd...

Calm down. You can't help Liz if you don't keep a level head.

"Deputy, I'd prefer you to face forward in your seat, please."

Tim's protests died unspoken at the cold smile on the man's face. With that gun to Liz's head, he held every advantage. His frustration level at a slow simmer, Tim turned around. The vehicle bumped up a shallow, snow-covered hill. Tim was thrown against the door as it jerked onto a narrow trail. He knew the place. Local access only. Used by the half-dozen or so folks who lived in the multimillion-dollar homes here on the back side of the mountain.

"Where are we going?" Jeremy's voice quivered, a sharp contrast to the steely tone that answered him.

"Well, that's for Miss Carmichael to tell us. I believe you mentioned something about a bank on the phone. Which one?"

His question met silence. For a moment Tim didn't think she was going to tell him. *Don't be foolish, babe. The man has a gun.*

Apparently Liz reached the same conclusion. "Farmer's Bank, on Walnut Avenue."

"And do you have the key to the safe-deposit box with you?"

Tim answered. "She doesn't. I do. It's on the ring Norville just took."

"Excellent. And the bank doesn't close until six o'clock. Plenty of time."

They drove in silence. Tim expected any minute to see flashing lights behind them. Surely the sheriff had mobilized the department by now, had followed him to the basement, checked outside the door, noted the fresh tire tracks in the new snow. Unless the traffic and the weather delayed him further. Tim tried not to think of the Friday-evening traffic that habitually packed Park City's streets.

They came to the end of the snow-covered trail and pulled out onto a main road. Jeremy merged into the traffic, and Tim's hopes dipped. Their trail was lost. Any hope of rescue rested with him now.

When they pulled into the bank parking lot, Cole directed Norville to park as far from the building's entrance as possible. Tim noted the security cameras mounted on the corners of the building. They'd pick up the vehicle, but were too far away to identify anyone inside.

"Now, here's my plan. Norville, you'll go with Deputy Richards into the bank, retrieve the Jersey Brooch and return. Miss Carmichael and I will wait here. Of course, it goes without saying that you will both act normally. Please don't give me a reason to harm this lovely lady."

Tim clenched his teeth. The man must be desperate. That "plan" was riddled with holes, except for one significant fact. As long as Cole kept his gun on Liz, Tim had no choice but to do as he asked.

"I expect this will take no longer than ten minutes."

As he got out of the vehicle, he caught Liz's gaze. She stared at him through red-rimmed eyes. Terror made her face white. Tim put as much confidence as he could into his smile before he closed the door.

He and Norville crossed the parking lot. As they approached the bank entrance, Tim held his palm out for the keys. When he had them in his hand, he spoke in a low, even voice. "I just want you to know, when we get out of this I'm going to wring your sorry neck."

He jerked the door open and strode through it, not caring whether Norville followed or not.

A line of customers waited in the queue to approach the tellers. Tim bypassed them, aware that Norville stayed on his heels, and went directly to the glass enclosure where the manager sat behind his desk.

The man gave Tim a half smile of recognition. "Hello again. Can I help you with something?"

"Yes, I need to get back into my box for a minute." Amazingly, his pleasant tone belied the anxiety churning in his stomach. "I forgot something this morning."

The man rose. "Certainly. Come this way, please."

Tim followed him to the vault. In vain, he looked for a chance to signal, to wiggle his eyebrows or mouth a plea for help. But whenever Norville wasn't in a position to see his face, the manager wasn't, either. Even when he signed in, Norville stood near enough to see what he wrote. Tim held his frustration in check. Liz's life depended on his actions. He had no choice but to follow the rules Cole had set out.

They had the silk box and were back in the car within their ten-minute limit. Tim twisted around in the passenger seat, held the box up in his hand and caught Cole in a hard stare.

"It's yours. As soon as you let Liz go."

The man's eyelids narrowed. "That's not how this is going to work."

The thumb on the hand that held the gun moved, and a loud

click sounded in the car as he cocked the hammer. A strangled sob escaped Liz's lips, and something wrenched inside Tim. She'd been remarkably calm through this ordeal. He wasn't sure he could have remained so calm with a gun held to his temple. He couldn't bear to do anything to upset her further, even if it meant sacrificing their best bargaining chip.

Without a word, he handed the box to Cole.

"Thank you. And now, I've got to keep you two out of sight until this is delivered to its new owner. Norville, head out 248, toward Kamas. Deputy, you might want to fasten your seat belt. The ride might get a little rough."

Tim did as he was told. The silence over the next fifteen minutes as the lights from Park City receded behind them was broken only by the noise of the tires cutting through the slush on the road and Liz's occasional sniffle. Outside, the snow eased to a few stray flakes and then stopped completely. They headed due east in a deepening gloom, the setting sun obscured by thick cloud cover.

"There's a narrow road to the right up here, Norville. Take that."

The vehicle left the highway with a lurch when Jeremy located the road. Tim had patrolled enough out here in the county to know this one. It wound around a couple of deep curves and through a narrow canyon. His courage nearly failed him. The area was riddled with abandoned mines. If they got too far off the main road back here, nobody would ever find them.

Jeremy slowed the Jeep to a crawl over the snow-covered road. If Tim's nerves weren't already stretched to their limits, this ride would have done it. In a couple of places, the vehicle slid and skittered on a steep section, but the tires managed to find purchase on the snow.

Finally, Cole directed him to stop. "We're going over there."

Tim looked where he pointed. He could just make out a dark

opening in the rocky mountain. "Are you crazy? That's an old mine shaft. We can't go in there. These things aren't stable."

"I know what it is. I've been here many times. In fact, I have some supplies stashed in the back, including some climbing rope that will come in handy for keeping you two under control for the next day or two."

Jeremy turned in his seat. "It's freezing out there and neither of them have coats. They won't survive till morning." He plucked at the sleeve of his jacket. "In fact, I'm not sure we will."

Cole, who wore a thick snowboarding jacket, lifted a shoulder. "We're not staying."

Jeremy twisted around and planted his hands on the steering wheel. "I don't like this. Why can't we just head back to your place, or even my place down in the valley? We can keep them quiet for a couple of days. Then you can hand over the pin, get out of town and everything will be fine."

Tim cocked his head sideways to level a disbelieving stare on Norville. Was the guy an idiot? Did he really think this maniac was going to let them go?

"Oh, yes." Cole's voice held derision. "Your plans have worked so well in the past." His door opened. The dome light cut through the gloom that had gathered inside the car. Tim caught Liz's frightened gaze. He smiled. *Don't worry. We'll get out of this.*

When Cole pulled her out of the vehicle, his smile faded. *I hope.*

TWENTY-NINE

A freezing wind whipped through the canyon and bit through Liz's shirt when she exited the vehicle. The setting sun was hidden behind the rocky cliff face that rose to her right. Dark shadows filled the canyon. She wasn't sure whether her quivering chin was from the cold or from the fear that gripped her with a cruel fist.

She'd been thinking hard all the way over here. Mr. Cole was ruthless. Her temple still tingled where he'd pressed the gun's barrel against her skin. They had to get away from him, but how? Since Jeremy told her the price the pair of brooches could command, she'd realized that Cole obviously was in this scheme for the money. Since he kept talking about turning the pin over to someone else, that meant he didn't own the matching piece or the proof of their authenticity. He was probably selling it to the person who did, and for far less than the five hundred thousand the pair could command. Could she use that to her advantage?

She gathered her courage before she spoke. "Mr. Cole, Jeremy told me about the Jersey Brooch, how much it's worth. I have an idea. My family isn't wealthy, but they're not destitute, either. I don't know what you're being paid for the brooch, but maybe they could match the price."

He actually chuckled as he motioned for Tim and Jeremy

to precede them toward a dark entrance in the rock. "A ransom? An intriguing idea, but I'm afraid I'll have to stick to my original plan. I've worked on the details for months."

Liz's sneakers sank into the soft snow on the path.

"Maybe we should listen to her," Jeremy said. "We could buy some time for both of us to get out of town. Her family would probably even pay more."

"There's only one problem. I don't plan to go anywhere. I've worked hard to position myself exactly where I am. The Jersey Brooch is merely a stepping stone, my ticket into an international organization that specializes in acquiring rare jewelry. It has been my master's trial, in a way, my final test." He patted the jacket pocket where he'd stored the brooch. "Which you, Norville, would have failed miserably."

Jeremy planted his feet in the snow and turned. Tim stopped, as well, and Liz was pulled to a halt by Mr. Cole.

"I'm getting a little sick of your comments." Jeremy's voice held the first hint of a backbone Liz had heard since Mr. Cole appeared. "I'm the one who told you about the stupid pin to begin with. I did all the research, even told you who owned the other pin and the sketch, so your mystery guy could get them. You didn't know anything about it until I told you."

Tim's gaze held hers. In his face she saw the realization of a harsh fact she'd just figured out. The three of them were not going to get out of here. Jeremy was the only one who didn't seem to understand that. Mr. Cole couldn't leave them alive, not now.

"You're right, Norville. I owe you an apology. You do have a few helpful skills." He released Liz's arm to pull something out of his jacket pocket. "Do me a favor, would you? Check to see if I've gotten any voice messages from my European friend."

He tossed the phone toward Jeremy, who caught it.

"Sure, I can—"

The world crashed to a halt as the gun was pulled away from Liz's head. A single heartbeat later, a shot deafened her.

Jeremy jerked backward and collapsed to the ground.

Tim leaped forward like a sprinter. Liz was knocked aside as he tackled Mr. Cole.

Beyond the ringing in her ear, a siren wailed. Flashes of red and blue bounced around the canyon walls.

On the ground beside her, Tim and Mr. Cole wrestled. Before the echo from the first gunshot had died away, a second blast tore through the air.

Horror exploded in her mind. "Tim!"

She was afraid to look. Snow soaked the knees of her jeans as she sank to the ground. Car doors slammed behind her.

Lord, please. Not Tim. I couldn't stand it if—

Strong arms surrounded her. A beloved voice whispered in her ear.

"It's over, baby. It's going to be okay."

The joy that stabbed through her was so intense it was almost painful. She threw her arms around Tim's neck. She was dimly aware of Jeremy's moan, and of a uniformed deputy running past her to kneel beside him, and of the man's shout for an ambulance. But she couldn't lift her face from Tim's shoulder. She never wanted to let go of him again.

Tim sat in the backseat of the sheriff's vehicle with Liz snuggled under his arm. Norville was going to have to wait until a stretcher could be brought into the canyon, but Sheriff Daniels wanted to convey Liz personally.

"I don't see why I have to go to the hospital," she complained. "There's nothing wrong with me."

"It's procedure," the sheriff told her. His eyes moved in the rearview mirror as he looked back at her. "You've been held hostage. You need to be checked over."

Tim relaxed into the seat and pulled her even closer. "Since we have a few minutes, I want to know how you found us."

"I sent somebody down to the basement to get you so I could chew you out for taking off by yourself. Found you missing, your weapon on the floor and the tracks outside. We lost your trail, but you told me this morning you were taking that pin to your bank. Easy matter to get somebody to pull up the payroll records and see where we deposit your paycheck."

Liz's head came up. "That was smart thinking."

The sheriff's head dipped forward to acknowledge the compliment. "We radioed, and you were spotted coming out of the bank by an off-duty deputy. Problem was, he was alone, and practically the whole department was at the other end of town at Eagle Summit. So all he could do was tail you and radio us."

Tim shook his head. "I never saw a tail."

"Johnson will like hearing that. We were less than five minutes behind you. Didn't know what the situation in that canyon was, so we were coming in slow and silent…till we heard the first gunshot."

Tim grinned at his boss's reflection. "You were a minute too late."

His grin was returned. "You seemed to have the situation under control."

"Does my family know what's going on?" Liz asked.

"Yes, ma'am. One of my deputies is bringing your parents to the hospital to meet us."

Tim was relieved to hear that. He'd be able to hand Liz over into the capable and protective hands of her father. And then there was an errand he had to run.

THIRTY

Three hours later, Liz walked through the entrance of Eagle Summit Lodge flanked by her parents. She'd not taken a second step inside when she was almost knocked down by an enthusiastic crowd. Jazzy, Caitlin and Debbie caught her in a group hug, squealing their relief, while Uncle Jonathan patted her back.

"Oh, Liz, I'm so glad to see you," Debbie sobbed in her ear, then held her at arm's length and looked her over with a worried glance. "Are you okay? Did they hurt you?"

"I'm fine," Liz assured her cousin. "Nothing more than a couple of bruises."

No sooner had Debbie released her than she was pulled into another embrace. Grandma squeezed with more strength than Liz would have given her credit for. "Elizabeth, my poor, poor girl. Can you ever forgive me?"

"Forgive you?" Liz returned her hug. "What on earth for?"

She leaned back to look the older woman in the face. Stress from the events of the past few hours seemed to have added a few wrinkles.

"Tim has been telling us all about the brooch." She shook her head. "It's all my fault. I should have waited to give it to you on your wedding day. Then that terrible boy wouldn't have found out about it, and none of this would have happened."

"That's ridiculous." Liz smiled to take the sting out of her words. "This is not your fault."

Grandma drew a shuddering breath. "If I had known what it was worth, I could have warned you. But I never had it appraised. I should have thought of that."

"Nobody thought of that. I've had the brooch for three years and I didn't think of checking on its value until somebody tried to steal it from me."

Grandma's heavy brow drew downward. "And to think we've been traced back to a…" She looked around, leaned close, and whispered, "to a notorious woman. We need to have that verified." Her chin rose. "I'd sooner think we came from the other line, the royal one."

At her side, Dad and Uncle Jonathan laughed.

Mom stepped up and put an arm around her waist. "Let's take Liz up to her room. She's bound to be exhausted."

Actually, she was. Her legs felt rubbery as she headed across the lobby. But she hadn't gone more than a couple of steps when Mr. Harrison came hurrying over from the front desk to meet her.

"Miss Carmichael, thank goodness you're safe." The man grabbed one of Liz's hands in both of his and actually brought it up to his lips. "We've been so worried."

"Thank you, Mr. Harrison."

"The police have taken Kate down to their headquarters for questioning." He hung his head. "I can't tell you how sorry I am for the part one of my employees played in your abduction. Unwittingly, I assure you. She didn't know."

"Of course she didn't." Pity for the man washed over her. "I just hope this isn't the last straw that sends Eagle Summit into bankruptcy."

He brightened. "Oh, that's not going to happen now. Just this morning we found a third-party investor, an avid skier who doesn't want to see the resort fold. We've already talked about hiring a consultant to minimize the damage and re-invent our image."

"That's great. I'm glad for you." Liz tried to sound happy for the man, but she'd caught sight of someone on the other side of the lobby. Suddenly she had trouble concentrating on Mr. Harrison.

Tim stood near the fireplace, speaking into his cell phone. As though he felt her watching him, he looked up. A flutter began in Liz's stomach when he disconnected the call and started across the lobby toward her, his gaze never leaving hers.

She needed to talk to him. Privately.

"Listen," she told her waiting family, "you go on upstairs. I'll be up in a minute."

Her mother's mouth opened. Before she could utter a protest, Dad stopped her with a hand on her arm. "Come on, Gail, Liz will be fine."

Liz shot him a grateful glance. He looked at Tim, and then winked at her before he pulled her mother away. The rest of the group left with them, Jazzy and Caitlin and Debbie all wearing silly grins. Their gazes bounced from Liz to Tim until they'd disappeared around the corner.

Liz met Tim halfway across the lobby. "Hi."

"Did everything check out okay? You're not hurt?"

"I'm fine." She stood before him, staring up into his face. She'd forgotten how easy it was to get lost in his eyes. With an effort, she looked down at her hands, which were clasping and unclasping like they had minds of their own. She whipped them apart and shoved them into her back pockets. "Listen, I wanted to talk to you about something."

"Yeah, me, too." He gestured toward the fireplace. "How about over there?"

She nodded. Now that she was alone with him, the words she'd planned while she sat in the emergency room had fled.

How could she ever explain why she'd hurt him so deeply three years ago? What could she say to excuse her behavior?

Nothing. There was no excuse.

She sank onto the couch facing the fireplace. Tim slid onto the cushion beside her and put an arm across the back. Not good. She couldn't think with him so close. But when she tried to lean back and put some space between them, she found herself leaning closer instead.

It felt so good to be with him. So right.

Her foot bounced with a fit of nerves. To distract herself as much as him, she asked, "So, do you think the sheriff will be able to find the man who was going to buy the Jersey Brooch from Mr. Cole?"

Tim shook his head. "He's not even going to try. He called the FBI and they're already on it. When he passed along the information Norville gave him, they sounded like they had a good idea who they're looking for."

Liz looked up, startled. "Jeremy gave them information?"

Tim's shoulders heaved with a silent laugh. "He's singing like a choir boy. Trying to cooperate in exchange for a lighter sentence. From what the sheriff has been able to piece together, Cole was planning to frame Norville for three murders—Sinclair's, mine and yours. He'd set up a meeting between Norville and Sinclair on the slopes right before he shot Sinclair, in order to place him at the scene. He put the body on the lift because he knew Norville worked as a lift operator in college, just like I did. Apparently, he thought that would increase the suspicion around him. Plus, Sheriff Daniels got a search warrant and searched Cole's apartment. They're still over there, but they found dozens of different kinds of locks, and some tools made of spring steel, so it looked like he'd been teaching himself to pick locks. Spring steel tools are used in clock repair, so he had some experience using them."

Liz remembered the clocks on the wall of the jewelry store. "But he wouldn't have gotten away with it," she said. "The sheriff knew about the Jersey Brooch. When they didn't find it on Jeremy, they'd know somebody else had it."

"Ah, but guess what they found on Cole's body? Two brooches. The real one and a copy. Not a bad copy, apparently. It wouldn't have fooled an expert, and probably wouldn't have fooled someone who has seen the real thing up close, like you. But it would have fooled the police for a while. And of course, with you gone, nobody would have known how long the fake had been in your possession." His arm slid off the back of the couch and he scooted closer to her. His breath felt warm against her cheek. "Let's not talk about that anymore. I want to talk about us."

His voice held so much warmth she couldn't breathe for a moment. She couldn't hold his gaze, but looked instead at the flames flickering in the hearth. Now was the time to tell him. If only she could remember the words she'd rehearsed.

Just spit it out.

"Tim, I am so sorry. I mean, for what happened three years ago with Jeremy." She swallowed. "I can't defend myself. I can only tell you that I've realized it was never about him. And it wasn't really about you, either. It was about me. I panicked. Suddenly, forever seemed like too long a commitment." She dropped her head. "I've asked the Lord to forgive me, and I know He has. But I need to ask your forgiveness, too."

He was silent for the space of five heartbeats.

"What about now?"

She risked an upward glance and found him watching her closely. "What do you mean?"

"Forever. Does it seem too long now?"

Liz's pulse stumbled. Could she be honest with him? She hadn't let herself be vulnerable with anyone in a long time, and it was scary. If she told him she'd realized she was still in love with him, he'd have every right to laugh in her face.

Flames reflected warmly in the dark depths of his eyes. Flames…and something else. Hope swelled in her heart. Was that love she saw shining in Tim's eyes?

Go ahead. Take a risk.

She leaned forward until her face was inches from his. Her whisper was almost a sigh. "Suddenly, forever doesn't seem long enough."

A smile teased the corners of his mouth. "Then I have a question for you. Would you consider taking this back?"

Without turning away from her, he reached behind him and pulled something out of his jacket. Liz looked down….

And gasped. He held her engagement ring.

"I couldn't get rid of it." His voice purred in her ear. "I never gave up hope that one day you'd come back to me."

The diamond swam out of focus as tears filled her eyes. She'd come to Utah to return a family heirloom that was never hers to keep. But tonight she'd received something far more precious in return. And she didn't intend to ever give him up.

She'd made her home on the other side of the country, but now Kentucky didn't seem much like home. Home, for her, would always be wherever Tim was.

"I'm back," she whispered against his lips. "For good."

With a delicious thrill coursing down her spine, Liz surrendered to Tim's kiss.

* * * * *

Dear Reader,

When my husband and I were dating, he tried to teach me to ski. Frankly, I'm surprised we ended up married. Liz's experiences with her friend Jazzy in chapter 13 are based, in large part, on our disastrous attempts to ski together. Only, Jazzy didn't cry all the way down the mountain, as I did.

Now that I've gotten a few years' experience under my belt—almost twenty—I love the sport. There is nothing quite like standing at the top of a snow-covered mountain, inhaling deep breaths of fresh air untainted by traffic and industry, and feasting my eyes on breathtaking vistas of God's handiwork as far as I can see. I know the Lord is with me always, but I'm acutely aware of His presence in a special way in the mountains.

If you have the chance to travel to Utah, I urge you to visit Park City. It's an old mining town with a delightful resort atmosphere, nestled in Utah's mountains and full of character. Park City, is, of course, a real place, but the businesses and the people in this story are all fictitious.

Thank you for reading *Murder at Eagle Summit*. I hope you'll let me know what you thought of my book. You can contact me through my Web site, www.VirginiaSmith.org.

Virginia Smith

QUESTIONS FOR DISCUSSION

1. Liz dreads returning to Utah because of her past mistakes. Have you ever avoided a situation that would force you to confront your past?

2. Tim not only held on to the engagement ring Liz had returned to him, he kept it on his dresser where he could see it every day. Why?

3. Debbie repeatedly defends Liz to their grandmother. What are the unresolved issues between Liz and Mrs. Carmichael?

4. Liz is reluctant to pass the brooch to her cousin. What personal significance does she attach to the heirloom?

5. Liz's friends support her in a variety of ways throughout the story. Identify and discuss them.

6. Grandma places a great deal of significance on the tradition of the brooch. How does this make Liz feel?

7. What was Jeremy's motivation for dating Kate?

8. What reason does Liz give for breaking off her engagement with Tim? How do you feel about her decision?

9. Given the rising divorce rate in our society, what steps should couples take to safeguard their marriages?

10. When the body is found, Mr. Harrison is concerned about how the discovery will impact his business. Is this a selfish reaction? Why or why not?

11. When Tim and Liz met, they immediately felt comfortable with each other. Tim attributes that in part to the fact that their families are so similar. When considering marriage, is it important to look at a person's family relationships?

12. Do you have any interesting family traditions, such as the Carmichaels' brooch?

*Turn the page for a sneak peek of Shirlee McCoy's
suspense-filled story,*
THE DEFENDER'S DUTY
*On sale in May 2009 from
Steeple Hill Love Inspired® Suspense.*

After weeks in intensive care, police officer Jude Sinclair
is finally recovering from the hit-and-run accident that
nearly cost him his life. But was it an accident after all?
Jude has his doubts—which get stronger when he spots
a familiar black car outside his house: the same kind that
accelerated before running him down two months ago.
Whoever wants him dead hasn't given up, and anyone
close to Jude is in danger. Especially Lacey Carmichael,
the stubborn, beautiful home-care aide who refuses to
leave his side, even if it means following him into
danger....

"We don't have time for an argument," Jude said. "Take a look outside. What do you see?"

Lacey looked and shrugged. "The parking lot."

"Can you see your car?"

"Sure. It's parked under the streetlight. Why?"

"See the car to its left?"

"Yeah. It's a black sedan." Her heart skipped a beat as she said the words, and she leaned closer to the glass. "You don't think that's the same car you saw at the house tonight, do you?"

"I don't know, but I'm going to find out."

Lacey scooped up the grilled-cheese sandwich and shoved it into the carryout bag. "Let's go."

He eyed her for a moment, his jaw set, his gaze hot. *"We're* not going anywhere. You are staying here. I am going to talk to the driver of that car."

"I think we've been down this road before and I'm pretty sure we both know where it leads."

"It leads to you getting fired. Stay put until I get back, or forget about having a place of your own for a month." He stood and limped away, not even giving Lacey a second glance as he crossed the room and headed into the diner's kitchen area.

Probably heading for a back door.

Lacey gave him a one-minute head start and then followed, the hair on the back of her neck standing on end and issuing a warning she couldn't ignore. Danger. It was somewhere close by again, and there was no way she was going to let Jude walk into it alone. If he fired her, so be it. As a matter of fact, if he fired her, it might be for the best. Jude wasn't the kind of client she was used to working for. Sure, there'd been other young men, but none of them had seemed quite as vital or alive as Jude. He didn't seem to need her, and Lacey didn't want to be where she wasn't needed. On the other hand, she'd felt absolutely certain moving to Lynchburg was what God wanted her to do.

"So, which is it, Lord? Right or wrong?" She whispered the words as she slipped into the diner's hot kitchen. A cook glared at her, but she ignored him. Until she knew for sure why God had brought her to Lynchburg, Lacey could only do what she'd been paid to do—make sure Jude was okay.

With that in mind, she crossed the room, heading for the exit and the client that she was sure was going to be a lot more trouble than she'd anticipated when she'd accepted the job.

Jude eased around the corner of the restaurant, the dark alleyway offering him perfect cover as he peered into the parking lot. The car he'd spotted through the window of the restaurant was still parked beside Lacey's. Black. Four door. Honda. It matched the one that had pulled up in front of his house, and the one that had run him down in New York.

He needed to get closer.

A soft sound came from behind him. A rustle of fabric. A sigh of breath. Spring rain and wildflowers carried on the cold night air. Lacey.

Of course.

"I told you that you were going to be fired if you didn't stay where you were."

"Do you know how many times someone has threatened to fire me?"

"Based on what I've seen so far, a lot."

"Some of my clients fire me ten or twenty times a day."

"Then I guess I've got a ways to go." Jude reached back and grabbed her hand, pulling her up beside him.

"Is the car still there?"

"Yeah."

"Let me see." She squeezed in closer, her hair brushing his chin as she jockeyed for a better position.

Jude pulled her up short. Her wrist was warm beneath his hand. For a moment he was back in the restaurant, Lacey's creamy skin peeking out from under her dark sweater, white scars crisscrossing the tender flesh. She'd shoved her sleeve down too quickly for him to get a good look, but the glimpse he'd gotten was enough. There was a lot more to Lacey than met the eye. A lot she hid behind a quick smile and a quicker wit. She'd been hurt before, and he wouldn't let it happen again. No way was he going to drag her into danger. Not now. Not tomorrow. Not ever. As soon as they got back to the house, he was going to do exactly what he'd threatened—fire her.

"It's not the car." She said it with such authority, Jude stepped from the shadows and took a closer look.

"Why do you say that?"

"The one back at the house had tinted glass. Really dark. With this one, you can see in the back window. Looks like there is a couple sitting in the front seats. Unless you've got two people after you, I don't think that's the same car."

She was right.

Of course she was.

Jude could see inside the car, see the couple in the front seats. If he'd been thinking with his head instead of acting on the anger that had been simmering in his gut for months, he would have seen those things long before now. "You'd make a good detective, Lacey."

"You think so? Maybe I should make a career change. Give up home-care aide for something more dangerous and exciting." She laughed as she pulled away from his hold and stepped out into the parking lot, but there was tension in her shoulders and in the air. As if she sensed the danger that had been stalking Jude, felt it as clearly as Jude did.

"I'm not sure being a detective is as dangerous or as exciting as people think. Most days it's a lot of running into brick walls. Backing up, trying a new direction." He spoke as he led Lacey across the parking lot, his body still humming with adrenaline.

"That sounds like life to me. Running into brick walls, backing up and trying new directions."

"True, but in my job the brick walls happen every other day. In life, they're usually not as frequent." He waited while she got into her car, then closed the door, glancing in the black sedan as he walked past. An elderly woman smiled and waved at him, and Jude waved back, still irritated with himself for the mistake he'd made.

Now that he was closer, it was obvious the two cars he'd seen weren't the same. The one at his place had been sleeker and a little more sporty. Which proved that when a person wanted to see something badly enough, he did.

"That wasn't much of a meal for you. Sorry to cut things short for a false alarm." He glanced at Lacey as he got into the Mustang, and was surprised that her hand was shaking as she shoved the key into the ignition.

He put a hand on her forearm. "Are you okay?"

"Fine."

"For someone who is fine, your hands sure are shaking hard."

"How about we chalk it up to fatigue?"

"How about you admit you were scared?"

"Were? I still am." She started the car, and Jude let his hand fall away from her arm.

"You don't have to be. We're safe. For now."

"It's the 'for now' part that's got me worried. Who's trying to kill you, Jude? Why?"

"If I had the answers to those questions, we wouldn't be sitting here talking about it."

"You don't even have a suspect?"

"Lacey, I've got a dozen suspects. More. Every wife who's ever watched me cart her husband off to jail. Every son who's ever seen me put handcuffs on his dad. Every family member or friend who's sat through a murder trial and watched his loved one get convicted because of the evidence I put together."

"Have you made a list?"

"I've made a hundred lists. None of them have done me any good. Until the person responsible comes calling again, I've got no evidence, no clues and no way to link anyone to the hit-and-run."

"Maybe he won't come calling again. Maybe the hit-and-run was an accident, and maybe the sedan we saw outside your house was just someone who got lost and ended up in the wrong place." She sounded like she really wanted to believe it. He should let her. That's what he'd done with his family. Let them believe the hit-and-run was a fluke thing that had happened and was over. He'd done it to keep them safe. He'd do the opposite to keep Lacey from getting hurt.

* * * * *

Will Jude manage to scare Lacey away, or will he learn
that the best way to keep her safe is to keep her close…
for as long as they both shall live?
To find out, read
THE DEFENDER'S DUTY
by Shirlee McCoy
Available May 2009
from Love Inspired Suspense

REQUEST YOUR FREE BOOKS!

2 FREE RIVETING INSPIRATIONAL NOVELS
PLUS 2 FREE MYSTERY GIFTS

Love Inspired®
SUSPENSE

YES! Please send me 2 FREE Love Inspired® Suspense novels and my 2 FREE mystery gifts (gifts are worth about $10). After receiving them, if I don't wish to receive any more books, I can return the shipping statement marked "cancel". If I don't cancel, I will receive 4 brand-new novels every month and be billed just $4.24 per book in the U.S. or $4.74 per book in Canada, plus 25¢ shipping and handling per book and applicable taxes, if any*. That's a savings of over 20% off the cover price! I understand that accepting the 2 free books and gifts places me under no obligation to buy anything. I can always return a shipment and cancel at any time. Even if I never buy another book, the two free books and gifts are mine to keep forever.

123 IDN ERXX   323 IDN ERXM

Name	(PLEASE PRINT)	
Address		Apt. #
City	State/Prov.	Zip/Postal Code

Signature (if under 18, a parent or guardian must sign)

Order online at www.LoveInspiredSuspense.com
Or mail to Steeple Hill Reader Service:

IN U.S.A.: P.O. Box 1867, Buffalo, NY 14240-1867
IN CANADA: P.O. Box 609, Fort Erie, Ontario L2A 5X3

Not valid to current subscribers of Love Inspired Suspense books.

**Want to try two free books from another series?
Call 1-800-873-8635 or visit www.morefreebooks.com**

* Terms and prices subject to change without notice. N.Y. residents add applicable sales tax. Canadian residents will be charged applicable provincial taxes and GST. Offer not valid in Quebec. This offer is limited to one order per household. All orders subject to approval. Credit or debit balances in a customer's account(s) may be offset by any other outstanding balance owed by or to the customer. Please allow 4 to 6 weeks for delivery. Offer available while quantities last.

Your Privacy: Steeple Hill Books is committed to protecting your privacy. Our Privacy Policy is available online at www.SteepleHill.com or upon request from the Reader Service. From time to time we make our lists of customers available to reputable third parties who may have a product or service of interest to you. If you would prefer we not share your name and address, please check here. ☐

LISUS08R